MURDER
IN THE
WPA

MURDER IN THE WPA

Alexander Williams

COACHWHIP PUBLICATIONS
Greenville, Ohio

To I. E.

Prologue

THIS AFTERNOON COCKTAIL PARTY at the Mayflower Hotel spilled over into another party somewhere in Chevy Chase in the evening. Both were exactly alike. Somebody—I've forgotten who—said, "Drop in, you'll see everybody you know." I didn't believe it, but it was so.

In the doorway I bumped into Ben Cook.

Together we said, "So you're here too."

"I'm a visiting fireman," I told him. "But I'm getting the urge. It looks like fun. And even some good work to be done. I wish I was in it."

Ben turned half around and said, over his shoulder: "Are you serious?"

I said, "Sure. I'm getting patriotic as hell."

"Come in and see me tomorrow," he called over two intervening heads.

"Where are you?" I yelled.

"Auditorium—first floor—ask anybody," he was half way across the room.

A man I'd never seen before in my life caught me by the arm.

"Old Ireton's got himself out on a limb, hasn't he." He wasn't asking me, he was telling me.

"Yes?" I acted wise. "How far out on what limb?"

"Well, I've heard tell somebody's going to bump him off if he isn't careful," said my informant.

"That's pleasant," I remarked. "Who is Ireton?"

From behind me a very nice deep-pitched feminine voice said, "He's my father."

5

She matched her voice. Almost as tall as I, she had black hair, and it may have been the smoke that made the glint of blue in it. Her eyes were a sort of dusty grey. She had a mouth, a noticeable mouth, that seemed well up to any purpose you could persuade her to use it for. And a chin. Her figure came off the front cover of a twenty-five-cent magazine. Altogether, Miss Ireton was one of those people you like to meet at cocktail parties. And afterwards.

"Tell me about your father," I invited. The anonymous gent slid away.

"If you're on WPA you know all about him," she snapped.

"Lady," I said, "don't shoot. I'm just a poor newspaperman trying to find out what it's all about."

"That's different," she said, and smiled enough to show how nice she could be if she really tried.

"My father came down with me yesterday," she volunteered, "but he had to fly back last night. I wish I'd gone with him. Everybody here is horrid. They all blame my father for things he can't help. I wish some of you wiseacres would try my father's job."

"Which is?" I prompted.

"WPA Administrator, of course," she said. "You don't mean you've never heard of him?"

"Now that you remind me, I do seem to have heard of him," I declared.

Then I suggested it would be a good idea if I wangled a couple of drinks. When I came back, with the glasses slopping over, she was gone. I drank both drinks, and plunged back into the maelstrom.

MESSENGERS AT THE PORTALS of the Auditorium next morning actually stopped talking to passing girls when I mentioned I had an appointment with Mr. Benjamin Cook. At the Auditorium, this was equivalent to unrolling a red carpet, getting down on their hands and knees, and bumping their foreheads on the ground three times.

Ben's secretary was sorry, but he was on the telephone. He was talking to the West Coast. That was normal. All high-powered Washington executives use telephones ambidextrously and dictate telegrams between them.

When I finally got in, I noticed Ben looked worried. People who know Ben won't believe this. He has the reputation of never worrying.

He is slow and calm. When everybody else is having jitters, he pulls out his tobacco pouch and loads his pipe.

He asked me, "What are you doing here, exactly?"

I told him I had a roving commission from the *Blade*, and was getting bored.

He said, "I need a guy who isn't afraid to stick his neck out, and won't get huffy if I have to fire him next week."

"You've hired a man," I told him. "How much do I get, and what's the job? And by the way, what exactly is this, anyhow?"

He said, "It's the Works Progress Administration. You know— the WPA. We're catching hell in Commodore Henry H. Ireton's district. Everything has gone wrong there and I can't find out what it's all about. Look over this wire from the Commodore. It came in this morning."

RECOMMEND WHITE COLLAR PROJECTS BE SEPARATED FROM REMAINDER OF WPA ACTIVITIES IN THIS CITY AND PLACED UNDER BUSINESS MANAGER STOP INCOMPETENT ADMINISTRATION PARTICULARLY IN ART MUSIC WRITERS AND THEATRE MAKES IT IMPERATIVE THAT STRONG CONTROL BE ESTABLISHED STOP THESE PROJECTS RIDDLED WITH COMMUNIST PROPAGANDA AND SUBVERSIVE ACTIVITY STOP REFUSE TO BE RESPONSIBLE UNLESS DIRECTORS ARE REPLACED OR DRASTICALLY DISCIPLINED AND MADE TO UNDERSTAND THEY MUST OBEY AND ENFORCE INSTRUCTIONS AND REGULATIONS OF THIS OFFICE

IRETON

Ben filled his pipe while I was reading this effusion.

"Well?" I said.

"It's all yours," Ben smiled. "Take it away. Take the rest of the day to get any material you can find around here, and catch a morning plane. I think there's one that pulls out around 7 o'clock. I'll drop in at your hotel tomorrow morning and pick you up and drive you out to the airport."

"What am I to be," I asked, "Pathé News? Sees all, knows all, and tells all?"

"Tells all," Ben admonished, "to me only. Go up there and keep me in touch. Write, wire, or telephone; but let me know every day exactly what the situation is."

"What of these projects he's complaining about?" I asked. "Are you going to do what he wants?"

Ben shook his head. "You'll have to find out for me. I don't know what to do. Ireton is pretty strongly placed politically. We can't afford to change administrators right now, and we can't afford to get in bad with the city officials and get messed up in local politics."

"How well do you know Ireton?" I asked.

"Pretty well," he said. "He's all right, but a terrible neurotic. He was in the Navy during the war, and he's a big shot in the real estate business. The Commodore is on account of his being a Commodore of the Yacht Club . . . There is something phony about this conflict between his office and the four Federal Art Projects. Find out what's underneath it all."

I said, "Okay, boss. See you in the morning."

ALMOST THE LAST THING that Ben said to me before I stepped into the plane was:

"Don't do anything positive until I tell you, but for heaven's sake be ready to act quickly and decisively as soon as you get the word to go ahead. This thing really worries me. There have been so many crazy threats, and so many ridiculous situations, I'm afraid that something terrible is going to happen."

"Cheer up," I said. "What is probably on your mind is a fore-knowledge that this damn plane is going to crash and get your ambassador all spoiled."

Without a smile he said, "I hope not. I haven't got anybody else to send up there."

1

WE WERE FORTY-FIVE MINUTES LATE, and we landed on a field like a marsh. Our gear slashed through puddles like a kid trying out a new pair of rubber boots. The hangars and the office were lost in gray, sodden drizzle and mist. They rolled the portable canopy up for us, but by the time we got under shelter we were all soaked.

I picked up a paper in the operations office, and took it into the bus with me. On the front page was a story:

RELIEF MARCHERS TAUNT ROOSEVELT
2,000 CIRCLE WHITE HOUSE CHANTING SLOGANS
AS DELEGATION PRESENTS WPA DEMANDS
GARNER REBUKES CRITICS
AT CAPITOL, HE DEFENDS POLICY OF PRESIDENT—
SIBLEY IS CONCILIATORY—PARADE ORDERLY

WASHINGTON.—More than 2,000 marchers, gathered here by David Lasser, president of the Workers' Alliance of America, paraded through Washington's downtown streets today, waving banners and chanting slogans, and presented petitions at the White House and the Capitol demanding increased appropriations for the Works Progress Administration.

The spirits of the marchers were undampened by a rain that threatened to spoil their "show," but the fifty local policemen assigned to escort them said that they had never handled a more orderly crowd.

The marchers, four abreast and extending for seven or eight blocks, obediently walked through the thoroughfares designated by the police, and broke the line wherever requested to facilitate the movement of traffic.

It went on for a column or more.

The bus from the airport landed me in the middle of town, and I took a taxi to the WPA Administration Building. I had my luggage forwarded from the airport directly to my hotel. Two blocks from the Administration Building my taxi was stopped by mounted cops. I stuck my head out into the drizzle and was told we could go no further.

"Why?" I asked.

"Them WPA workers is havin' a demonstration," the officer told me.

"How do I get into the building?" I asked.

"Nobody's allowed through these lines without a pass signed by Commodore Ireton," I was informed.

I produced my brand new blue official card. The mounted officer eyed it doubtfully.

"I'm from Washington. I flew up this morning for a conference with Commodore Ireton," I explained. "I've got to get into the building."

The officer looked over my credential card again.

"Federal man, huh?" he said.

"Yes," I told him. "Who's in command here?"

A policeman was standing on the curbstone, his black slicker dripping, listening to me try to sell the mounted cop on the idea of crashing the lines. A big man in a civilian raincoat, his hat pulled down over his eyes, came up and both cops snapped to attention. I leaned far out into the rain and yelled:

"Hey, Pete!"

Lieutenant Pietro Tonelli, in civilian clothes, recognized me. It's no compliment; he remembers everybody. He waved his hand and came over.

"Hiya, kid," he said. "You covering this story?"

"No," I told him. "I'm in the army now."

"Whaddya mean, army?" he demanded.

"Same thing," I explained. "I'm working for the WPA. I just got in from Washington on the morning plane."

I paid off the taxi, and with Tonelli walked the remaining two blocks to the Administration Building.

Wet, miserable relief workers were touring an endless chain around and around the block. The police had formed them in a column, four abreast, and they plodded, their heads bent, their coat-collars turned up as a partial protection against the rain. The men looked stupid, sullen and beaten. The women were bedraggled and wet, but their heads were up and they gave the impression they were enjoying themselves.

Policemen held every point of vantage.

"You must have every reserve in the city on the job," I said to Tonelli.

"Look," he pointed.

They were repairing the street in front of the Administration Building. It had been cobbled, and they were laying asphalt. The torn up cobbles were piled in neat pyramids and squares along the edge of the curb.

"Can you imagine what would happen if one of these lugs got the urge to start heavin' that Irish confetti around?" Tonelli asked.

On the corner in the partial shelter of a doorway, Police Commissioner Joseph P. Hardy, an inspector, and a couple of captains of police tried not to look worried. Tonelli marched me up to the brass hats and halted me there.

What Benjamin Cook had forgotten was that I had once been a newspaperman in this town. I knew a lot of people, among others Commissioner Joseph P. Hardy. I hated him from his gardenia down to the soles of his custom made boots. He thought as much of me. Still, the chances are that Ben hadn't forgotten at all. He's a cagey lad. He figured that I would have a good enough in with people who could tell me things, to counterbalance the bad effect of those who were hep to me and my style.

"Good morning, Commissioner," I said in sugary accents.

He growled, "Are you back in town? I haven't got anything to say. You can see for yourself everything is peaceful. The police are doing their duty. There are no rough tactics—"

"What about the cobblestones?" I asked. "When do they start to fly?"

He looked scared. "For God's sake don't suggest it."

I laughed. "I'm not a newspaperman any more. I'm an official just like you are, only not so important, of course. It's part of my job from now on to help keep down ructions."

Tonelli passed my official identification card over. The Commissioner read it with a "say it ain't so" expression.

A shrill-voiced girl broke ranks and trotted at the side of the huge picket line. She waved her hands above her head, and began chanting:

"GIVE THE BANKERS HOME RELIEF! WE WANT JOBS!"

The whole mob took it up. Hardy bent over and yelled in my ear:

"What the hell is a WPA Federal Coordinator?" He stabbed at the title on my identification card with a disgusted forefinger.

"Me!" I yelled back. "I'm a trouble shooter! I coordinate! I cut out red tape! Make things move faster!"

Hardy handed back my card—at least he started to, and then passed it over to Tonelli.

"They certainly picked the right man for the job if they wanted trouble," he said nastily. Then to Tonelli, "Take him through the picket line and stand by until the lobby guard finds out if Commodore Ireton wants him on the premises."

I followed the billfold. It had all my money in it, my travel authorization, and my identification. The money was the important thing, though. It takes a minimum of three weeks for the Government to okay and pay an expense voucher. Even then it's money on consignment. The Comptroller-General's office has been known to call you on the carpet after a lapse of five years and demand to know why you charged railroad fare at $4.61 when there was an excursion that day at $2.59.

"I haven't seen you since you got your step," I made conversation with Tonelli. "How does it feel to be a lieutenant?"

"All right," he said.

"Sort of tough doing this work. I mean being away from the Homicide Squad and all the excitement, isn't it?" I asked.

"I'm still on the Homicide Squad," he assured me. We turned into the building. "I'm here today because every available man is needed."

Seven lobby guards took a gander at my card, and finally after much telephoning Commodore Ireton's office admitted there might be a man named James Moore from Washington. I snatched my billfold from Tonelli and took the elevator to the eighth floor.

For a moment I thought I'd got into the morgue by mistake. The elevator landed me in a short corridor which opened into a room about fifty-by-fifty, formed by ten-foot-tall wood and glass partitions. There were eight or ten guards at the elevator, and the reception room had its doors guarded by two or three men each. In the reception room, on the bare concrete floor, at least a hundred people were laid out flat on their backs in rows.

There was ample time to take this in while my card was being examined again. It passed from hand to hand, ending in the custody of an official—and when I say official, I mean official.

His red, white and blue necktie was under one ear, and he wore no vest. His coat met over and above a bulging belly, and was held straitly by the center button. His shirt rucked out of his pants in scallops, and his belt buckle had a strained and worried look as if each breath might bring the ultimate disaster. In his coat lapel he sported the greasy ribbon of some foreign decoration. He chewed gum and breathed forth a mixture of garlic and spearmint, and his wide-brimmed black hat made him look like a chef masquerading as a Congressman from the Blue Grass.

It had become plain that the rows of people on the floor were not dead. They shifted and turned, and occasionally even groaned.

"What's going on here?" I asked dumbly. Guards and officials like dumb people. They understand them.

"Sit-down strike," one of the guards answered.

I let my eyes run along the row of men and women stretched full length on the concrete.

The guard answered my gesture. "They been here since las' night. They're kinda tired," he explained. "They've given up sittin' for layin'."

"All of these people have been here since last night?" I wanted to be sure my information was correct.

"This is only the half of 'em," he boasted. "Some got sleepy, some got hungry and thirsty, and some hadda go to the johnny. Once they go out, they stay out. They don't get back in, see?"

The man who had my card fixed me with his off eye and stuck out a chunky fat paw with a surprising grip.

"I am very, very glad to meet you, Mr. Moore," he said. He had a vaudeville accent, and when he smiled his teeth showed as snaggles. "How is my good friend Mr. Ben Cook in Washington?"

I got my hand away from contact with him as quickly as I could.

"*Is* he a friend of yours?" I asked, allowing my doubt to be apparent.

"Mr. Benjamin Cook is my long-time friend," he assured me. "Any friend of his is a friend of mine. You follow me, I'll take you inside."

We stepped carefully between the rows of men and women on the floor. They hardly noticed us. In my topcoat pocket was a package of life-savers and a couple of sticks of chewing gum. I dropped them on the chest of the last man I stepped over, and it was something like dropping breadcrumbs into a pool of hungry pike. One of the door guards growled and started for me, but my guide held up his hand.

"It's all right," he said. "This is Mr. Moore from Washington."

"Aren't you allowed to feed the animals?" I asked.

The WPA Administration Building was originally built as a warehouse or loft building. Offices had been partitioned off around three sides of the floor, which eliminated all daylight from the large center space. My guide slanted over toward a door at the left-hand side, marked ADMINISTRATOR. Another door on that side was marked CONFERENCE ROOM. Directly ahead in the back wall was PUBLIC INFORMATION. I knew that to be the office of Danny Mulroy, the publicity man. Twenty-five or thirty other offices opened into the central space, with the reception room blocking the passage to the passenger elevators. It was a big building.

Herded in a corner by the Information office, in a roped-off space, stood a group of about fifty men and women. Fifteen or twenty guards marched around them and kept them bunched, like cowboys riding herd.

My guide jerked his thumb toward them.

"How long have they been there?" I asked.

"Since before nine o'clock this morning," he answered.

It was past three then.

"Are there no benches or chairs for them to sit on?" I demanded.

"They can sit on the floor if they get tired. They don't have to wait if they don't wanna," he grinned.

He ushered me into the outer office of the Administrator with pomp and ceremony.

"Mr. Moore, from Washington," he announced.

Behind the desk facing the door sat a good-looking woman secretary. She was a knockout except for black circles of weariness under her eyes and worry wrinkles between her brows.

She stood up wearily. She had forgotten how to smile.

"The Administrator will see you right away," she said. "He wants to talk with you before he goes into conference with the directors of the Art Projects."

Her office was an anteroom to the throne. It had three doors. One opened outside; one, on the left, into the Administrator's office, and one, at the right, led into a conference room.

She opened the door at the left and announced: "Mr. Moore, Commodore Ireton."

My official guide up to this point backed toward the outside door. "Glad to have met you, Mr. Moore," he smirked. "Anything you need while you're in town, just ask me. Jones is the name. Izzie Jones. Maybe you heard of me?"

"Sure," I said. "I've heard of you. Thanks."

"Thank *you*, sir," he said and tried to bow, but his belly wouldn't let him.

Behind me the door of Commodore Ireton's office closed. His desk was placed slantwise, across the corner of a big room, between two windows, one of which overlooked the side street and the other faced front.

"Good day, Mr. Moore," came his voice.

With all the weird stories told about this man, nothing had prepared me for his voice. It was like a bull rhinoceros in pain. It had depth, but it was weak and squeaky at the same time. Rich in timbre, but high pitched.

His face was a mass of contradictions. He had a broad brow with thick curly hair only slightly white at the temples. His eyes were green in that gray, greasy, mid-afternoon light. The lids were heavy and drooping. His nose was thin and high-humped at the bridge with a long droop at the tip, and with arched nostrils. His upper lip was thin and stretched tight, the lower one full and curved. The whole head was pear-shaped, broad and noble at the temples, dwindling down into a narrow, mean, intolerant chin.

While I walked toward his outstretched hand extended over the desk—the limp, ready hand of a politician—I saw all this, and the American flag ostentatiously drooping on its standard to his right and behind him.

"Ben Cook asked me to come in his place, Commodore," I told him. "He's tied up in a series of conferences and couldn't get here until next week at the earliest."

He dropped my hand and motioned toward a chair.

"He thought maybe I could help get this situation in the Professional and Service Division ironed out," I went on in my best and most ingratiating manner. His desk was piled high with reports. Sheaves of them. Some of them so bulky they were tied together with heavy manila wrapping cord. He opened sheaf after sheaf as he talked, snipping the cords with a long-bladed pair of office shears.

"I could straighten it all out in five minutes," he screeched in that eldritch voice. "Tell Cook to let me fire half a dozen of these recalcitrant, incompetent, subversive, maundering, sniveling, bawling, misbegotten, alligator-hided, Communistic directors he's appointed to these Arts Projects. With them out I could have everything under control before you could snap your fingers."

There was nothing to do but grin.

"They have good records in their fields," I tried to soothe him. "Some of them haven't had much experience as administrators—"

"Administrators," he yapped. "Ha-ha-ha. They don't run their projects. The projects run them. And the Reds run the project employees. The whole setup is riddled and stinking with propaganda direct from Moscow."

I continued to try and smile it off.

"They aren't Liberty Leaguers, but after all artists are bound to be liberal in—"

"Liberal my eye," he cut in. "They're a lot of Goddamned Reds!"

The secretary put her head in the door and said, "Commodore. The guard captain is here and says this delegation which has been waiting for you all day is getting impatient. Couldn't you see them now? It will only take fifteen minutes."

He screamed, "No! I'll see 'em when I get damned good and ready to see 'em."

"Some of them look mighty tired and hungry," I said. "Couldn't you see them now?"

He snarled at me. "Why should I see 'em? I didn't ask 'em to come here. They're a lot of no good—"

He went off into a long stream of invective and foul language. It got under my hide.

"They're human beings," I snapped. "And you're a public servant. You have no right to keep them waiting this way."

"Who's the administrator here?" he yelled. "You or me?"

"You are, Commodore," I said. "But it might be a good idea for you to remember that even administrators are perishable. I think you're playing with dynamite. I'm not presuming to tell you your business, but it doesn't help to make desperate people angry and vengeful."

He barked at me, "Young man, you take care of yourself and I'll take care of myself. I haven't reached the spineless stage of some others in this government. By God, sir, I've fought with *men*, and I'm not going to cringe before these mangy Red paupers."

"In far more elegant language," I reminded him, "Marie Antoinette said about the same thing. And she found out."

"So you've come up here from Washington to threaten me," he thundered. "This is another overt threat. Well, threaten. Threatened men live a long time. I get three or four notes every day telling me somebody's going to bump me off."

"If I were you, I'd watch my step," I warned. "In Washington they are uneasy for your safety."

The door opened, from the secretary's room, and a girl came in. The same girl I'd seen at the party in Chevy Chase.

"I hope I'm not interrupting official business, Father," she said. She looked beyond me.

"Nothing important," he answered.

I said, "How do you do, Miss Ireton. I hope you remember me?"

She looked me up and down. "I remember you very well. You were with the gang of hoodlums in Washington who were making nasty remarks and threats about my father. I suppose you have come here to *spy* on him?"

"Oh, no," I said. "I came here because I could not forego any longer the pleasure of your charming conversation. You say such nice things to people."

"I do to nice people," she countered.

2

WHILE COMMODORE IRETON and his daughter went into a personal and domestic huddle, I looked out of the front window. Eight stories below, that endless column of fours flowed along the sidewalk in the drizzle. Now and then they would raise their voices in some sort of a slogan, but the general impression was of a parade of marionettes.

Miss Ireton's pleasant contralto with its special cutting edge for me said, "Good day, Mr. Moore." But when I turned she was leaving the office. I looked expectantly at the Commodore, who pressed a button on his desk. When Miss Hirzner popped in he said:

"Are the Art directors still waiting?"

When she said yes, he dragged himself to his feet. His face was bluish, and he looked like a mighty sick man to me. I followed him into the Conference Room where the directors were slumped around the long table. I knew most of them.

Mrs. Mabel Flood, local director of the Theatre Project, was medium of height, slim and dark. She looked like an actress. A good second-lead in a first-rate stock company. She was competent. She knew plays, knew the history and the meaning of drama.

Joseph McMurray, local head of the Music Project, was a fine 'cellist, a distinguished musician, but he had an idea he was a good conductor, which he was not. Fortunately he had sense enough to leave administrative details of his project to his assistant, who was a businessman and an accountant.

Harry Gruening, director of the Art Project for the region, had a reputation as an art critic, and affected a van Dyke beard. He was young, lazy and erratic, but a swell guy. He fought for his project like a tiger. He would lie, steal, doublecross, play politics, do anything to give his artists a chance to make a living and do their work.

Bennington Graeme, head of the Writers' Project, was an ex-newspaper and magazine man. One of the best drinking companions in the known world, he could turn out good copy on almost any subject, and he made his boys and girls toe the line. In his job he had to be good. So many writers are psychopathic cases.

In addition to the Arts directors, there was at the table Matthew Van Gelder, who headed a small project which employed a lot of research workers and folks with legal training. They were making an index and a survey of the legal and historical papers in the vaults and the repositories of the city. There was also a woman whose name I didn't catch, a faded middle-aged blonde who had something to do with the women's division; and a Captain Treadfast, who was in charge of some branch of personnel. He was on detail from the Engineering Corps of the Army, and was not enjoying the detail any too much, judging by the savage way he chewed a cigar.

I didn't attempt to greet any of the directors. I stood at the head of the table with the Commodore while he presented me ungraciously. Everyone present was anxious and strained, sensing a crisis. To them I was another unknown quantity. They had got to the point where they expected nothing that was good. To them, another emissary from Washington was another bird of ill omen.

Somebody shoved a chair in my general direction, and Ireton leaned against the table and cleared his throat in a platform manner. Without any apologies for keeping them waiting, he plumped into the middle of the fray.

"Ladies and gentlemen, we've come to the parting of the ways. You and I no longer see eye to eye. Something must be done, either you or I must yield an untenable position."

"We never knew you had taken up a position," Bennington Graeme muttered. Ireton ignored him.

"There are two points of view represented here," the Administrator continued. "There are some of you who feel that you are directly responsible to the Federal authorities in Washington. I feel that I cannot continue to do justice to my responsibilities unless I have complete control in my own district. I feel that the work relief program is the responsibility of the community. The people on the relief rolls are citizens of this city, they have been supported by the taxpayers of this city, and in spite of the fact that we are now receiving considerable aid from the Federal Government, I still believe the city is primarily responsible for the well-being of the WPA workers in its boundaries."

This looked as if it were going to be a long oration. I lighted a cigarette and settled back to wait until something more potent and debatable was said.

During a pause, we could hear ourselves breathing. We were all keyed up. I had been absorbing tensity from that atmosphere ever since I left my taxi . . . Ireton began again. He said something, some cliché or generality, that nobody ever heard. Outside sounded a single scream, followed by a chorus of yells, screams, and shouts. A terrific crash, as though the building had collapsed, and then a hullaballoo of shrieking, yelling, stamping, scuttling, mauling, crazed men and women.

I jumped for the door. All of the people at the table sprang to their feet as panic communicated itself to us. Only Ireton stood as if he were planted. I saw him lean slowly over, support himself on the table, and then turn and walk very slowly, tottering, in the direction of the door which led through his secretary's office to his own sanctum. I yanked open the outer door of the conference room, and almost simultaneously Miss Hirzner opened the door of her office next door and peered out. She was ghastly white. Ready to faint. I took a step toward her, and then was too busy to think of her any more.

The delegation that had been standing like cattle all day to talk to the Administrator had gone berserk. A woman had keeled over. Then a couple of other women became hysterical, and in a moment they were beyond control. The guards tried to restrain them. Struggling and fighting, the mass of them smacked into one of the high office partitions and it went down in a splinter of yellow pine and crashing glass. Some few people were trying to raise up the edge of the partition to pull victims out from under it. Nobody appeared to be much hurt, but all the pent-up venom in the crowd was loose. A flying wedge of guards, with my friend Izzie Jones at the head, went into action.

In the waiting room the sit-down strikers came to life and began their own little riot. They drove their guards into the open space before the offices. I stepped into the thick of it, into the midst of a Donnybrooke free-for-all. Women, tears streaming down grimy faces, mixing rouge and mascara in inky rills, clawed and kicked at guards. Men hit out in any and every direction. The guards began to swing their clubs. Blood was flowing. The babel was terrific, the high loft ceiling threw back every echo three times enlarged.

Directly before me a woman, her hat hanging to a few hairs in the miraculously erratic manner of female headgear, struggled away from a guard. Her high, run-over heel kicked out and caught him in a sensitive place in the shinbone. He squeaked and grabbed, and she kicked again at a more vital spot. She was no lady. Her kick hurt. He yelled again and his right hand reached swiftly for his hip pocket. He had turned and was backed in front of me, two steps away.

Reaching behind him for his hip, his right wrist was in the perfect position for a hammerlock hold. I moved in on him, caught his right hand, and forced it upward between his shoulder blades. His fist was clutching his gun. I said in his ear, "Take it easy, buddy," and put a little more pressure on the hammerlock. He spun around, dropping the gun which I caught as I backed away. He started a haymaker for my jaw, but I sidestepped and then he got a good look at the muzzle of the gun pointing at his diaphragm. His enthusiasm cooled instantly.

"What's the matter, don't you feel so tough without your gun?" I asked him. He came at me again.

I shifted the gun to my left hand, and stiff-armed him with my right. I caught his ugly mush fair, and he went staggering back into the press of rioters. Somebody clipped him, and he found too much to do in other directions to care about me.

Swirling arms and striking fists, men and women getting up and going down, a flash of a ripped coat, somebody pulling hair, a man trying to stanch a bloody nose, a guard throwing away a billy that had cracked in half. A jagged rip in a man's trousers-knee, showing the bleeding abrased flesh underneath. No tailor could ever mend that rip so it wouldn't show.

Then, just like the movies, came the bluecoats and brass buttons. Tonelli was with them. The elevators spewed them out, and they looked good. The WPA guards were not in uniform. That griped me, I can't say just why. It seemed wrong for men in civilian clothes to be clubbing other civilian men and women, even in the interests of preserving law and order. The cops were another matter. They moved in, doing their stuff. They knew there was more hysteria than viciousness in this mob. They were almost benevolent in the businesslike way they edged the crowd in a body toward the exits.

One burly copper caught up the heavy rope that had penned in the delegation. He took one end, and his partner took the other. Then they walked around the edge of the crowd, using the rope to round up the whole gang. In that kind of a mêlée one seldom looks down, one keeps his glance high. The whole lot could have wriggled under that rope, if they had thought to do it, but they didn't think. Those on the outside of the press felt the rope at their waists and instinctively moved away from it, pushing those on the inside in the direction the cops wanted them to go.

The objectives of the police were two freight elevators at the extreme end of the floor. With everything under control, the door of one of these was flung open. Inside was a motor police patrol. It backed right out on the floor. The police expertly cut out the worst of the fighters, shoved them in the wagon, and slammed the grille on them. Then the patrol wagon drove back on the elevator, and down to the street. That little episode made headlines on Page 1. It was attributed to the tactical genius of Police Commissioner Joseph P. Hardy, in personal charge of the forces of the law. Hardy actually took good care not to stick his nose into the eighth floor of the WPA Administration Building until all the fighting was over.

Danny Mulroy, the short and square—in more ways than physical—WPA publicity man, sidled toward me from his office.

"Going to get out a news release on this, Danny?" I asked him.

He said, "What do *you* think." He put his lips close to my ear. "At that," he whispered, "the Old Man *would* get out a news release if I'd let him."

I said, "Sure he would. I can dictate it to you. 'The Federal Projects are overrun with dangerous Reds. This demonstration is only one of a great number of overt acts, which proves their resistance to the forces of law, order, and decency.'"

"That's about the gist of it," Danny said.

I said, "Damn Red-baiter. He's getting everybody in a jam. Can't you muzzle his trap, Danny?"

A silly looking slug wearing a guard's badge along with a beautiful black eye, sidled up beside me and looked expectant.

I said, "Here's your plaything," and handed him the gun I had taken from him in the scuffle. "You better get someone to tell you how to use this thing. And until you learn, you better leave it at home. You'd better leave it home anyway. You're too sensitive. Get your wife to practice kicking you in the shins at home."

He took the gun away from me. "You'll hear about this," he growled.

"Yes," I told him, "no doubt I will. And if you keep on flourishing that gun you're going to be hearing some nasty remarks from the District Attorney when you face a manslaughter rap."

Danny went into the Administrator's anteroom, and I moved in that general direction. Bennington Graeme, standing with a couple of other people from the interrupted conference, said to me:

"That's a nice stiff-arm you've got, Jim."

My fingers and wrist were sore.

Tonelli came ambling by, winked, and began to oversee the efforts of three or four men to raise the fallen partition.

"Nice entertainment you have here," I congratulated him.

"Can you imagine it?" he said. "That partition went over, and all that glass smashed around, and not a soul badly hurt."

"Probably there are three dead men under the wreckage," I said cheerily.

The Commissioner of Police made his grand entrance then, flanked as usual by his brass bats. Tonelli in duty bound moved over to make his reports to the great man.

Bennington Graeme said to me, "Look at the Commish. Guess he stayed out in the rain to keep his gardenia fresh."

"Anybody with brains could make a good wisecrack about it being too stuffy in here for a stuffed shirt," I said. "You figure it out, Benny, and I'll feed a come-on line to you some day when you can make a gag that will enhance your reputation as a wit."

He said, "Thanks, pal."

By this time all of the conferees except the Commodore were in a loose group of which Bennington Graeme and I were the focal point.

"I suppose," this was Mr. Van Gelder speaking, "the conference is off for the afternoon."

Harry Gruening said, "I'm going to make a protest to Washington. This sort of thing cannot continue. Did you see those people in that delegation? Some of them were from my project."

"They were from all the Arts Projects," Bennington Graeme informed us. "Lawrence Parsons was heading the delegation."

"Is Larry Parsons on WPA now?" I asked. And then I remembered. He had been fired from his job for too much activity in organizing a chapter of the Newspaper Guild.

Just then Danny Mulroy came hurrying from the far end of the floor by the elevators and turned into the Administrator's office. I hadn't seen him leave the office, but he evidently slipped out. There was a muffled yell from inside, and Danny popped back out again. His mouth was opening and shutting like a goldfish. He managed to croak:

"Izzie! Izzie Jones! Come here, quick!"

Izzie, from some unseen quarter, came on a waddling trot. Bennington Graeme and I, out of sheer curiosity, went too. Bennington said, "What's up, Danny?"

Mulroy pointed inside the Commodore's office. He, Izzie, Bennington Graeme and I all pushed through the door at once. The Commodore was not immediately visible. His chair was overturned, and he was sprawled on the floor. Around his neck was wrapped tightly, so tightly it had cut into the soft skin, a double strand of wrapping cord. A piece of the cord that had been tied around some of the reports on his desk. His eyes were bulged out, his swollen tongue protruded from his mouth.

He was dead. Very dead.

No man's face could be that color purple, and he still live.

Dead bodies are all very well in their place. I've seen plenty of stations and undertaking establishments, hospitals and morgues. If I know I've got to look at a stiff, I can rib myself up to it. But this was nasty. It was sudden. I felt very guilty. I felt that but for the grace of God, I might have wrapped that cord around his neck myself.

I went over in the corner by the bookshelves, and was very ill.

3

FOR THE FIRST and, I hope, the only time in my life I had to take the wrong end of a police grilling.

It got to be half past eight, and nine o'clock, and then half past nine; and still it went on and on. We conferees were all there, suffering and sweating. The police had no easy job. Even the gardenia Commissioner Joseph P. Hardy affected wilted after a while. The one mitigating circumstance was Lieutenant Pietro Tonelli of the Homicide Squad from Headquarters.

Pete did his stuff quietly and efficiently as always, and let Commissioner Hardy be the front man, as it is laid down in the unwritten manual of the police force. Commissioners come in from civil life not knowing a yegg from a teletype, but immediately they get the grand build-up and take the credit from the men who do the work, like Pete. We had moved into the Conference Room, and were all around the table: Hardy at the head, Pete Tonelli alongside of him, Mrs. Flood and McMurray at the opposite end of the table; Danny Mulroy, Harry Gruening, Bennington Graeme and myself, in the order named, on the right hand side of the table; Matthew Van Gelder, Miss Curtain—she was the gal from the women's division—and Captain Treadfast on the other side of the table.

Sarah Hirzner, Commodore Ireton's secretary, had been allowed to go home; in fact, Tonelli had sent one of his men with her in a police car. That was the polite way of keeping tabs on her until she was needed. Pete believed in tact where possible.

The Commissioner was having a hard time getting us straightened out in his mind, and finding out what we did and why. The inquiry had found out a lot more about WPA than the murder, so far. You couldn't blame the Commissioner. After all, WPA is a complicated setup, even under normal conditions; and with a murder in the next room, it was a combination of Lewis Carroll, Edgar Allan Poe, and Gilbert K. Chesterton, all paradoxes and nonsense unless you had the key to the riddle. The Commissioner didn't know from nothing.

"Now let me get this straight," he said for at least the tenth time. "You, Mrs. Flood, are director of the Theatre Project."

She nodded. She looked as if she had been out on a nine days' bat without any sleep.

"And you, Mr. McMurray," the Commissioner commenced the weary rounds, "are head of the Music Project. Mr. Gruening is head of the Art Project. Mr. Graeme directs the Writers'—"

I broke in.

"Van Gelder is the director of a research project, Miss Curtain is from the Women's Division, Captain Treadfast is Personnel, Danny Mulroy is a dirty press agent, and I am a scoundrel from Washington. You can call me what you like, but what do you say to something to eat? And about nine large, cold bottles of beer?"

Beside me Bennington Graeme groaned, "Must you talk like that?" Tonelli licked his lips.

All in all, they continued to get exactly nowhere very fast. Of the ten of us in that room, at least nine, and more likely all, had blared severally and individually in public and private that we hated Ireton's guts. Any one of us might have been in his office. Any one of us might have murdered him, for good and sufficient reason. Any one of a hundred or more of the rioters might have done it. For that matter, it could have been Izzie Jones. And I, for one, was in favor of that notion. Without the exact figures of the total enrollment of WPA for the district, it is hard to state a number; but if there were a hundred thousand or two hundred thousand on the payroll, that is the number of suspects there were in Commodore Ireton's murder.

Sarah Hirzner had gone completely to pieces at the first few questions. That's the reason they had let her go. Those leading questions, few as they were, established Ireton as the great hated of all time. To more specific questions she swore that nobody had passed through her office into Commodore Ireton's office. That she would have seen them, if they had. I piped up to say that somebody might have gone past her when she looked out at the riot; and she denied point blank that she had looked out. I asided to Graeme, "Who's she covering up, I wonder." Hardy must have thought the same, and pressed her for a better answer. She burst into tears and began moaning:

"It was the Commodore's cursing. That horrible, terrible cursing. He cursed everybody. He said dreadful things to people. No wonder he was killed. I knew somebody would get him. I warned him that somebody would fly into a fit of rage some day and kill him. But he would not stop cursing."

Hardy and then Tonelli tried to get her back on the track, without success. Then Hardy said:

"*Who* do you think would kill him?"

She went completely haywire. She broke into a babble that didn't mean anything, which finally tapered off into a wailing cry over and over again—"Cursing . . . cursing . . . cursing . . ."

Pete Tonelli stepped in then, whispered something in Hardy's ear, and sent her home.

"Was that an act she was putting on?" Graeme whispered.

"I don't know," I whispered back.

Tonelli said sharply, "Please do not talk in whispers. If you have anything to say, say it out loud so the Commissioner can hear you."

As nearly as we could figure it out, when we heard the crash outside of Ireton's office we had all started for the door together. As I remember it, I was the first one out of the conference room; but I may not have been. I could not swear to it, and neither could anybody else. Mrs. Flood remembered that she and McMurray had gone out together. McMurray remembered going out with Mrs. Flood, and Gruening—but Gruening thought he went out with Alice Curtain and Captain Treadfast. Actually, we all jumbled into the doorway together and nobody ever could decide who went out in what order and who stayed back, as far as our testimony was concerned. We should have been fine witnesses. We were all supposed to be above the average in mental capacity and observation powers, while actually all we contributed was a fine picture of our own confused minds.

What with trying to get us in proper official categories, and trying to make head or tail of what we said, and did, in those few minutes before the murder, Hardy severely overtaxed *his* none too brilliant mind. It was beautiful to watch him floundering and to compare his clumsy, ineptly phrased questions with the occasional crackling, clean cut queries that Tonelli rapped out. The Commissioner was a great help to the Lieutenant in a negative way. He would drone along until the witness was lulled into complete unguardedness, and then Tonelli would flash a crucial question and surprise answers that were valuable and honest.

Although Tonelli said very little, he took a lot of notes, and every once in a while he would get up quietly and send a man of his off on an errand. I had forgotten how he worked. He followed his own line and made his own deductions, but that was in a sense off the record. There were always two Tonellis working: the one a brilliant man, the other a policeman who covered the case in that thoroughly stupid, unimaginative and absolutely complete manner in which the police do cover cases of this sort. It is that meticulous attention to obviously stupid things that gives the Detective Bureau so good a record of arrests and convictions. The system makes it almost impossible for a routine criminal to escape, and keeps the unusual criminal on the hop.

Tonelli had none of Hardy's worries. Tonelli could be all cop, but Hardy was both cop and politician. Hardy was unable to determine in his own mind if we were or were not big shots. If we were important Government officials, he was treading on very thin ice. Indeed, most WPA officials are confused on that issue. Each considers himself a big shot; but it is a moot question. WPA is a world apart and ordinary yardsticks will not measure it. Fifty years, say I, then it will be known whether it was good or bad. It will probably be here then too.

Izzie Jones wandered in and out, full of business and importance. He would whisper in Tonelli's ear. He scribbled countless notes and put them in front of the Commissioner. In between times he would leer reassuringly at anybody whose eye he could catch, and disappear again.

At half past nine Hardy chucked in the sponge. He rose and said:

"You will all have to consider yourselves as material witnesses. I will exact from each of you your promise that you will not leave town and that you will hold yourselves in readiness for questioning any time the Department may require."

Tonelli had our names, telephone numbers, and addresses. I tried to get his attention, but at the moment he was strictly business, friendly with no one of us. We milled around for a few moments, not quite knowing what to do with freedom now that we had it; and then, scarcely speaking a word, we got our hats and coats. Bennington Graeme and I were last to start for the elevator. I had a strange feeling there was something wrong somewhere, something lacking. There was something I should have, which I didn't have. But my mind was so intent upon food and beer that it didn't matter greatly.

"Did Hardy leave something out, forget something?" I said to Graeme.

"Handcuffs, maybe," he said grimly.

The big space outside the offices was strangely quiet and deserted. There were still guards at the doors, guards at the elevators, guards everywhere, and a couple of workmen puttering at the wreckage of the partition. As Bennington and I passed, one of them turned and spoke to me.

"Jim," he said softly.

I looked at him hard. It was Lawrence Parsons.

I said, "My God, Larry, what are you doing here?"

"Can you get me out?" he asked.

I said, "Sure, I can get you out. Come on. Did *you* bump off the Commodore?"

"No," he said. "All I bumped was my head when that damned partition fell on me."

I said, "Well, you would lead the delegation from the Arts Projects."

We were close by the guard at the door then, and kept our mouths shut. The guards looked us over, one asked, "Are you three gents together?" Bennington Graeme and I both said yes. Apparently the guard didn't know how many people had been in the conference room, or who might leave and who couldn't. We didn't enlighten him, but got into the elevator.

In the lobby there was a slight delay. They had brought Commodore Ireton's body downstairs, and the stretcher blocked the entrance. A radio car swung up to the curb, and out of it flopped Miss

Ireton, supported by a cop. The Commodore's body on the stretcher was close behind me. She took one look at the covered form, rushed over to it, lifted the sheet and bent over her father's face. White-faced she turned away, saw and recognized me, and in termagant fury, attacked.

"You!" she said in a low intense voice. "This is your fault. You were sent up here to kill him."

The policeman with her grasped her arm, pulling her away. She was set to slog me. Bennington Graeme thrust himself between us.

"You're nervous and overwrought, Miss Ireton," he said. "You don't mean what you're saying. I'm perfectly certain that Mr. Moore had nothing to do with your father's death."

"*You're* certain?" she lashed out at him, still in that intense, deadly voice. "*You're* one of the gang too! You wanted to see him dead! It's a plot. You're *all* in it. And *I'll* see that you're exposed. I have ways of getting to the truth."

Larry Parsons had pulled away, run out on us. He was giving a good imitation of a disinterested bystander. He stood far over on the edge of the sidewalk, half sheltered by the radio car that had brought Miss Ireton.

Nothing Bennington Graeme or I could do or say to the girl would appease her. I tweaked Graeme by the sleeve and he followed me, with the girl staring after us.

The pickets had gone. The police drove them away when the rioting started inside the building. Bennington and I walked across the avenue where only a few policemen mounted guard, and hailed a taxi. Larry Parsons came slinking up and Graeme held his nose as if Parsons was a bad smell.

"Hello, rat," he said. "Fine guy you are, leaving two poor defense-less men at the mercy of a wild gal."

"I had my reasons," Larry mumbled. "I didn't want to be conspic-uous with all the cops around."

That made sense.

I said, "Come on, get into the cab." I gave my hotel address to the driver and then said to the boys:

"So you're both in the WPA now."

Bennington Graeme piped up, "Be your age. Everybody's in the WPA now."

The last time I saw Lawrence Parsons was at Flemington, when we were both covering the Lindbergh kidnapping trial. Larry was star man for the *Globe-Democrat* then, and I was working for the World Affairs Press Syndicate.

Bennington Graeme knew Larry as well or better than I did. We ribbed the lad a bit, but we saw his side of the picture. It doesn't pay for delegation leaders to stick out too far when they don't have to. Too many people would be glad to see them in jail.

Larry told us that he'd headed this delegation to Ireton, after he had tried to persuade them not to go. He said he knew Ireton would be lousy about seeing them. They had all got hungry and tired and more sullen and angry as the minutes and hours went by. When the girl had fainted, Larry said the rest began to push him and shove him, and that he was directly under the partition when it went over. It was lucky he was not killed. It was equally lucky he had been stunned, he commented. The police arrested all the rest of the delegation, but nobody found him under the wreckage. When he had pulled himself out, the main riot was at its height.

"I crawled on my hands and knees," he said, "into the Conference Room. And then I went through into Ireton's secretary's office."

"Was she there?" I asked him.

"She was hanging out of the door watching the riot," he said. "I was still a little groggy, but I wanted to tell Ireton what I came to tell him. I opened the door into his office."

"Did you tell him?" I asked.

"Hell, no," said Larry. "He was as dead as a fish."

I said, "Says you."

He shrugged. "I am quite capable of killing him," he said. "I never did like the bastard. But I didn't do it. Somebody beat me to it. Now you see why I don't want to answer police questions. They'd be sure to pin it on me."

"Maybe it was me," said Bennington Graeme. "I don't know; ask me."

"It's all settled," I said. "Miss Ireton blames me."

The cab pulled up in front of my hotel. I reached for money—and then I knew what it was that had been worrying me back there before we left the Administration Building. That cockeyed Izzie Jones had never given me back my wallet. That's what I had missed.

Bennington Graeme paid. He thought it was a new stunt I'd worked out to get my taxi fare paid. Nobody expected Larry Parsons to pay, not even himself. How could he on tuppence a week? That is the rate of pay for a first-class newspaperman in the WPA, with hundreds glad to get it.

The hotel had my luggage and they had assigned me a room, as per telegraphic request. We three went upstairs together, and I got Room Service. Then I put in a call to Washington. After some forty minutes of hunting they located the Honorable Benjamin Cook at a cocktail party in Silver Springs. He came on the phone to say:

"Good lord, couldn't you call me tomorrow morning?"

"It was too good to keep," I told him. "Somebody has just killed Ireton."

He said, "How the hell can you afford to stay drunk on Government per diem allowance of five dollars?"

"I've just made a deal with the telephone company," I explained. "They're giving me a kickback of ten per cent on my telephone calls. As soon as I finish this report, I'm going to call North Dakota, and talk for an hour and a half."

"What *is* this?" Ben asked. "Are you being humorous?"

"Not very. I'm trying to tell you," I explained. "I arrived here, had a fight with Ireton, went with him to a conference of the Arts directors, and during the conference a riot broke out."

Ben said, "That's not news. Ireton's conferences are always riots."

"This wasn't Ireton's riot, it was some of the project employees," I said. "It seems they don't like being laid off. Will you call the attention of the proper authority to that? So, while we were having a merry time taking guns away from each other, somebody slipped in behind our backs, wound a piece of string around Ireton's neck, and killed him."

Ben spoke sharply: "That's the second time you've said that. Do you mean it?" I had got under his skin.

I said, "Ireton's in the morgue, as you predicted he would be; all of your local Arts directors and I, your coordinator, are under arrest. And in your report for the day you might mention that Miss Ireton thinks her father was killed on instructions from Washington brought here by me."

There was a lot of confusion on Ben's end of the wire. A girl's voice yelled, "Why don't you come over? It's a swell party!" Ben came back on the line.

"There's too much noise here. I still don't know whether you're drunk or sober—but if you're drunk, you're fired!"

I said, "You can't fire me. The police want me to stay here."

Beefsteaks and beer appeared. I signed the check. Graeme and Parsons took it for granted they were invited to dinner.

The telephone rang. I said, "This must be Ben." But it wasn't. It was the desk. The clerk said a *gentleman*—and he emphasized the word—who *said* his name was Jones, was downstairs and wanted to see me. I said I'd go down and see him. Izzie was one of the few people to whom I really wanted to talk at that moment; and I didn't want Bennington Graeme and Larry Parsons to cramp my style by being present at the interview.

Izzie bobbed and smiled and bowed as polite as a Japanese customs inspector. He was all apologies. He was *so* sorry. He had forgotten to return me my wallet. Here it was. Would I please count money and look over the papers and be sure that everything was intact? I did just that, slowly and carefully, as insultingly as possible. Everything was there.

"What's the idea?" I said.

Izzie bobbed and smiled and apologized some more. "Just an oversight," he insisted. "I overlooked returning it in the excitement."

"Not that," I snapped. "Who killed Commodore Ireton? Did you?"

"I never in all my life murdered a man, I assure you," he said earnestly. "I have killed some, in action; but I do not murder."

I said, "Why not?"

He said simply, "I am afraid. I do not want to go to jail. I do not want to go to the electric chair. It is a very bad thing to kill men, in civilian life."

"What did you want to tell me?" I asked him. "You held out on this wallet for some good reason. What was it?"

He didn't bat an eye. "I thought it might be convenient at this time," he said, "to speak to you confidentially."

I said, "Okay. Go ahead."

"A lot of things are happening," he confided. "I thought Mr. Benjamin Cook should know about them."

"Ben Cook knows all about everything," I said.

"Mr. Benjamin Cook is a very fine man. A wonderful man. A scholar, a gentleman, and"—Izzie sank his voice to a stage whisper—"I know a great deal about him. He is very liberal in his political views."

"So you think Ben's a Red?" I kidded.

Izzie was horrified.

"I did *not* say that," he protested. "He is a liberal. He is also my friend. He believes in justice for the working people. I believe in justice for the working people. We are both liberal. Never believe if people tell lies about me. I am liberal."

"What have you got to tell Ben?" I demanded.

"It is about the Fascist organization," he said in his most conspiratorial tone. "Commodore Ireton was encouraging them. They have an organization in the WPA. They have a general, they have an admiral, they have chiefs of divisions, they have a general staff, they have headquarters, and a secret password. And all of this organization is being done on Government time, right in the office of the Administration Building."

"How do you know so much? Are you chief of their intelligence service?"

He dug into his back pocket and produced a battered, worn pocketbook. From it he extracted a sheaf of approximately fifty cards. Some of them were union memberships; some were lodge cards. They were in English, German, Yiddish, Russian; I got glimpses as he sorted them over and selected one. This he held up proudly, shook it over my head, not letting me have it in my hand.

"I am not the head," he said. "I am only a member."

What could I say to that? I sat down and motioned him to a seat beside me. I said:

"Start at the beginning, Izzie, and tell me *all*."

Before Izzie Jones had finished, I accumulated an amazing respect for the man. He was undoubtedly a colossal liar. I am sure he
was thoroughly and unmorally un-honest. There is no doubt he was
a soldier of fortune of the lowest order. Whoever would and could
pay him, could hire his services. Yet with all of it he had a strange
loyalty of his own, and a code of ethics he only could follow. What it
could be, I'm not prepared to say. He was perfectly capable of working for two people at the same time whose interests were inimical.
Perhaps his saving grace was that everything was secret, and that
he told everybody everything he knew or could guess. When I say
everybody, I mean of course everybody who could in any possible
way reward or aid Izzie. He had no time to waste on underdogs who
showed any chance of remaining permanently under. This, mind
you, was an outsider's estimate of the man. It does him too much
and too little justice.

He had it thoroughly grounded in his mind that I was a left-
winger; and therefore he did his best to present every political fact
in a manner that would either alarm me or flatter me, accordingly as
he interpreted it. To hear him talk you would think him a bosom pal
of Stalin's, yet he boasted the ribbon he wore in his buttonhole had
been presented by General Denikin in token of his loyal services to
the Russian White Guard.

If I stretch Izzie out at full length it is because I want to give
Izzie full credit. Tonelli did the spade work. I tagged along and asked
questions. But Izzie was inspired. Had Conan Doyle known Izzie,
Sherlock Holmes would be fat. Had Edgar Allan Poe known him,
Poe would have been a humorist and drunk himself to death years
before he did.

According to Izzie the WPA in the district was a kind of colossal bear garden wherein roamed all the prize nuts of the political
and social science world. Every lame duck who couldn't get a job
anywhere else had been appointed to some high sounding executive
post. The official figures show that only 2% of WPA appropriations
was spent for administration, and there is no reason to doubt those
figures. But from Izzie's point of view, and from what I saw of the
picture, that 2% was so active it multiplied itself a thousandfold.

Every kind of 'ism, cult, creed and fancy was incorporated some-where in a WPA project. And in spite of all this, or maybe because of it, the rank and file did a good job, wherever they got half a chance.

I got Izzie down to brass tacks. We went over the list of the sus-pects in the murder, and began to eliminate those who looked un-likely to us. Lawrence Parsons was so obviously guilty he couldn't possibly be. Captain Treadfast was only an Army engineer. I could imagine him shooting, clubbing, strangling with his bare hands; but never with a cord. That shows too much imagination for a slide-rule boy. Izzie, however, ingenious and ingenuous at once, pointed out that Captain Treadfast had done a tour of duty in Cuba. The garrote is a favorite method of murder in that island. Izzie's theory was that an engineer might learn and adapt even with a limited imagination. I applauded Izzie's ingenuity, but nevertheless crossed Treadfast off my own personal list. I eliminated myself, but I'm perfectly certain Izzie did not. Sarah Hirzner I eliminated; at which Izzie looked wise, started to tell me something, then changed his mind. Alice Curtain, of the Women's Division, I crossed off, Izzie concurring. That left us with the five Directors—and none of them seemed unlikely.

I argued that people do not kill for purely academic reasons, but I didn't quite believe it. No matter how much you may differ with a man over matters of administrative procedure, I said, you don't kill him to convince him. But while I said it, I could not laugh off the hysteria that prevailed in WPA. At that moment I didn't know the complete picture. I discovered very rapidly that insofar as the WPA was concerned, administrative procedure was an extremely personal matter, a fighting and a killing matter. Men lived, died, and were reborn over the placement of a comma.

Remembering my guests upstairs, and hoping that they had not availed themselves too liberally of Room Service, I went to the desk and called to find how they were making out. No answer came from the room. I went up, and they had both left. For no good reason, I brought my hat and coat down when I came back. I said to Izzie:

"Mr. Graeme came in with me, but he has grown tired of waiting, and left."

Very slyly Izzie said, "Yes. I saw you leave the Administration Building with Mr. Graeme and Mr. Parsons, but I do not remember that Mr. Parsons came into the Building with either you or Mr. Graeme. Mr. Parsons also drove here with you and Mr. Graeme."

I said, "Do you know when he did come into the Administration Building today, Izzie?"

Izzie grinned again slyly. "Yes," he said, "he led the delegation of the art projects."

"If you knew that, and you saw him leave the building with us, why didn't you have him arrested? That's your duty, isn't it?"

"It is not always good policy to have a suspect arrested immediately," said Izzie.

I said, "Are you having him tailed?"

"No," said Izzie calmly. "Lieutenant Tonelli is attending to that."

I took off my hat and wiped my forehead.

"Am I being tailed too?"

"Oh, yes." Izzie was quite cheery about it. "So am I. We're all being tailed."

I said, "Nuts. Let's go have a drink."

"Would you like to see Mr. Graeme again now?" Izzie asked.

I wasn't particular, but I thought I'd find out what Izzie knew and what the boys did after working hours. So I said, "Very much. Where is he?"

"He is attending a party," Izzie informed me. "There will be some people there you know. Why don't you go?"

He began to creep under my hide.

"How do you know there's anybody there I know?" I demanded.

Izzie said, "Commodore Ireton liked a lot of information. He was particularly interested to know what the art directors were doing. I can tell you the personal habits, the friends, acquaintances, and background of every one of them."

"Why do you work?" I asked him. "With what I guess you know about these people, they should be willing to support you in handsome style to keep your mouth shut."

"That would be blackmail," said Izzie piously.

I pushed him into a taxi. One thing could always be counted upon with Izzie: if a crime had a name, Izzie wouldn't commit it.

I spotted the house in which the party was by the percussions which made the front walls bulge. Outside it sounded as if they were beating dishpans. Izzie said he wouldn't come up, but I thought I'd better have a look-see. I hadn't had enough noisy parties for one day. I managed to wedge my way through the door into the kind of brawl short story writers call "typically Bohemian." There were fifty people jammed into a room designed as dwelling space for one couple. Six or seven of them were from newspapers; four or five did advertising or department store personnel. Most of these I knew. In addition there were a lot of familiar faces, hangers-on in pubs around town, one or two professed poets and "serious" writers. There were three or four sailors, a huge, bulking brute of a man who turned out to be a longshoreman, and a whole bevy of those females who used to wear batik blouses and who think perfume is a substitute for baths. Oh, yes, and Bennington Graeme, as foretold.

Indeed, the party hung on Bennington. He was the center, the sun of this universe. As head of the Writers Project, he was either the boss of, or had the power to give jobs to, eighty-five per cent of the people present. He was *not* pleased to see me.

A crushed muslin sort of woman with the gray-blue eyes of a drowned kitten informed me she was the hostess. I said I was a friend of Bennington Graeme, and was crashing the party; and she said that was fine. There was gin and there had been ice, she murmured in her distrait, detached manner, and there might be oranges and lemons. Anyway, there was gin, and would I like some. I said no, but I'd drink it. Over in one corner a girl with longish black bobbed hair, dressed in a tweed skirt and a boy's sweatshirt with a Mickey Mouse stenciled on the front of it, announced in a husky voice that she wanted to hear poetry—some of Charlie's poetry. I gulped my gin hastily. If I had to hear it—and only God could stop Charlie from declaiming his poetry—I needed fortification. There was a little dissent, but gradually the idea took hold. Came vociferous demands for Charlie. I nigh onto choked on my second beaker of gin when Charlie got up. He was the big hulking longshoreman.

My hostess, whose name I never discovered, crept under my elbow and said Charlie was so interesting. Somebody had discovered him in a beer joint opposite the docks. Charlie was reading aloud from the funnies to one of his friends, and the discoverers realized at once he was a poet at heart.

I wriggled over to Bennington Graeme and asked him, "Is Charles on the Writers Project?"

Bennington jumped as if I had broached a State secret.

"Don't mention it," he whispered. "He wants to get on the Project, but I haven't got a spot for him. I dodge him day and night, sleeping and waking. He says he's a poet, therefore why can't I *make* a place for him. That's what they all think. They believe if I don't give them a job it's because I personally don't like them."

In a raspy baritone Charlie, from the middle of the floor, declaimed:

"Turgid and sullen are the River waters. Grapefruit rinds bob slowly, up and down beneath the piers, and little boys swim naked among them."

There was a hell of a lot more of it.

When Charlie had finished, everybody applauded vigorously, with Bennington Graeme, the hypocrite, yelling, "Bravo!"

I got another drink of gin, and eased out as Charlie began another deathless bit about some rats in a warehouse. Izzie was waiting at the corner. After Charles, Izzie's face looked wholesome and honest.

There didn't seem to be anything to do but go home then. Izzie was very disappointed when he left me. He was sure I was holding back on the events of the party. He panted for nice, fresh, inside information on the machinations of the Communist party as revealed in wild confessions stimulated by the atmosphere of gin and nameless sin. Izzie's idea of that kind of party had been formed in youth from Hearstian Sunday features. No matter what he saw and heard for himself, he always believed this romantic business was going on. That parties could be dull and lead to nothing but headaches he would concede only for suburban use. Wild parties with *artists* had to be different.

I persuaded the night clerk to get me some magazines from the news stand which was closed, and tottered off to my room to read in bed. It was near one o'clock.

Why I should have thought I could get rid of Izzie that easily, I don't know. About quarter past two, just when I'd decided to turn off the light and go to sleep, he was on the telephone.

"Allo," he said. "Is this Mr. Moore?" Izzie's dialectical faults were amplified by telephone.

I said, "No."

"Mr. Moore, no kidding," he said, "I'm at the hospital."

I said, "Good."

"But *I* am not hurt," he said, indignant at my lack of feeling. "It is Mr. Graeme."

"What's the matter with him?" I asked.

"They are not quite sure," said Izzie, "but they think his jaw is fractured, and maybe his head. It is almost certain he has a broken leg, and one broken rib. And then he was almost drowned, and he is suffering from cold and exposure."

"Don't break the news so gently, Izzie," I said. "Give it to me all in a lump. I'm strong. Did somebody set fire to the party, too? How many people were burned to death?"

"Oh, no," said Izzie blandly. "It was only Mr. Graeme who was nearly drowned."

"I suppose the decent thing for me to do is to come over there," I said resignedly.

"Oh, no," said Izzie again, "that would do no good. Mr. Graeme has been given a shot in the arm, and is asleep."

"That's fine," I said. "I don't want to be decent, I don't like to be decent. Good night, Izzie. Don't call me again unless you get killed yourself."

"But I couldn't—"

I hung up on his protest.

With the pillow punched into place, and the bedclothes pulled out from around the edges so as to keep my back warm, I opened the windows, padded back to bed, and had my hand on the light switch when the phone rang again.

I said into the transmitter, "Go away, Izzie."

Pete Tonelli said from the other end, "Oh, well, if you don't want to hear about this—"

"I know," I said. "Bennington Graeme's in the hospital. So what?"

Tonelli chuckled. "Thanks for the news," he said. "They haven't reported that to me yet. I called to tell you your other little playmate is in jail."

I said, "What little playmate?"

"Lawrence Parsons," said Pete. "You know, the fellow you passed out of the Administration Building this afternoon."

I said, "My God, does every fly cop in town know about that?"

He said, "There's two out in the sticks that might not."

"Well," I said, "why did you wait till now to put him in the jug?"

"We didn't put him in the jug for the riot this afternoon, nor yet on a murder rap," said Tonelli. "We are holding him on a charge of being a nuisance and loitering."

"Where did he loiter?" I asked.

"Mostly," said Pete, "outside Commodore Ireton's house, but partly in the corridor of the house, near Miss Ireton's bedroom."

"Honestly, Pete," I said, "I don't know what's got into you. There used to be a time when you wouldn't pinch a guy for trying to make a girl."

"I don't mind," said Pete, "when the guy knows the girl."

"How do you know she didn't know him?" I asked.

"That's what she says," said Pete.

"What does he say?" I asked.

Pete said, "He doesn't say nothing. And a great deal of it."

"Is that any reason," I asked, "why you should call me up?"

Pete tried to sound injured. "Well, I just thought you'd like to know."

"You mean," I snarled—I was belligerently sleepy by now—"that you thought I'd spill something. Well, I don't know anything to spill. I'm not smart and holding out on you, Pete. I'm dumb and ignorant. Good night."

4

MAYBE I SLEPT TWENTY MINUTES. Then I woke up and lay there think-ing of Larry Parsons in the coop, until finally I got goosepimples all over and thought I might as well get dressed as lie there and suf-fer. Someone could do a swell tract on the close connection between goosepimples, hives, indigestion and conscience.

It was a satisfaction to wake up Tonelli, and badger him until he agreed to go down to the jail with me. A jail is a lugubrious place. It's not so cheery in the daytime, and at three o'clock in the morning it's the personification of the heebie-jeebies.

My good deed proved to be its own reward, which so seldom hap-pens I want to get it in the record. If I'd waited until next noon to call, Larry would have got his second wind and would have been defiant. As it was, we caught him just right. He was in the midst of the high despondency of his first night in jail. We thought he was going to cry, he was so glad to see us. The fool had refused to tell his story when the police took him, and he was not very much more inclined to talk to Tonelli and me.

He did break down enough to admit that the Commodore's daughter was not a complete stranger to him.

Tonelli asked, "How did you happen to meet Miss Ireton?"

"I met her on the job," Larry admitted.

"What job?" I asked out of turn.

Tonelli gave me a nudge, which meant for me to keep my mouth shut. Larry considered carefully.

"I guess it won't do any harm to tell you this," he said solemnly. "When I went on the Writers Project I had half-finished a play. I happened to mention it to Bennington Graeme, and he encouraged me to hurry up and get it finished. He told me he'd turn it over to Mabel Flood for production by the Theatre Project, if it was any good. When the play was finished, Mrs. Flood liked the idea, and it finally got into rehearsal. I began spending a lot of time at the theatre, naturally, this being my first play. Then Commodore Ireton brought his daughter over to the theatre one afternoon, to show her how the wheels went around."

I said, "By the way, Larry, what is Miss Ireton's first name?"

"Her name is Jane Esmerelda. But her friends call her Jaze for short."

Tonelli choked over his cigar, and I had to give myself a mental pound on the back. Larry went serenely on. He's a handsome lad, but humorless. He'll be a great success as a playwright. Every joke will be labelled and no one will be bothered by the fear of laughing out of turn.

"Girls are kind of funny," he said modestly. "Jaze was a bit stage-struck, and when she found out I was a playwright she thought I was wonderful."

"I'll bet she thinks you look like Gary Cooper, too," I said.

Larry had the decency to blush. "No," he corrected, "she thinks I look like Freddy March."

"And what do you think of her?" I said to Larry. "No, don't tell me, I know: freckles like Myrna Loy, body by Harlow, and a mind like Sappho, George Sand, and Portia, all rolled into one."

Larry nodded. "While Papa was fussing around the theatre that first afternoon, raising hell with everybody," he said, "I made a date with Jaze; and we've been seeing each other ever since."

"Then what was the reason for the second-story act tonight?" Tonelli asked.

Larry shrugged. "I didn't think it'd be so good if anybody saw me at that house," he explained.

Tonelli said, "Is that so? Of course you knew Miss Ireton wasn't at home then."

Larry looked a little worried.

Tonelli leaned back in his chair. "You might as well come clean," he said. "We know a lot about what went on last night. I suppose it would be a great surprise to you to know that Miss Ireton was rounded up with the rioters from outside her father's office and taken to the police station and held there until she had identified herself."

Larry didn't look so surprised.

I chimed in, "How did that happen? She was in her father's office not fifteen minutes before the riot, and I saw her leave."

Tonelli gestured toward Larry. "Maybe *you* can explain," he suggested. "Maybe you'd *better* explain—unless you want to get your girl friend in bad."

"I can explain," said Larry. "Jim is right. She came out of her father's office about fifteen minutes before the riot started. She saw me with the delegation waiting to see the Commodore."

"She didn't by any chance know you were coming down there, and just drop in on the off odds that she would see you?" I asked.

Larry admitted I had called the turn.

"We have to do that sort of thing," he said. "You see, we couldn't let the Commodore know anything about our knowing each other."

"Let me get this straight," said Tonelli. "Miss Ireton knew you were going to be at the Administration Building with a delegation. She came down there on the pretext of seeing her father, but actually to see you. She stopped and talked to you on her way in to see her father, I suppose."

"Yes," said Larry.

"How long?" Tonelli demanded.

"I don't know," said Larry. "Fifteen or twenty minutes, maybe a half hour."

"It's a hell of a place to hold hands," I interposed.

Tonelli went on with his questioning. "Then she went into her father's office and stayed there a few minutes. Then she went back and talked to you some more?"

"That's right," said Larry.

"And she was with you when the riot started."

"No," said Larry. "She had left me. I thought she had got safely out of the building."

Tonelli grunted.

I said to him, "Give, Lieutenant. How did she happen to get caught in the roundup?"

Tonelli said, "She was waiting for the elevator when the fuss began. Somehow she got swept back into the main riot when the sit-down strikers in the waiting room and the guards got into the shindy."

Larry put in, "I wouldn't know anything about that. I was under the partition at the time. I was pinned under it when it crashed down."

Tonelli asked: "How do you account for the lady not remembering who you were when we asked her if she could identify the prowler in her house?"

"I suppose," Larry said, "she wanted to continue to keep it secret that we know each other."

Tonelli grunted one of his expressive grunts.

To give Larry a chance to think I said to Tonelli, "I don't understand anything about this. You say Jane Esmerelda was caught in the roundup and taken to the stationhouse."

"Sure," said Tonelli.

"Then," I said, "how come, why, when did you talk to her?"

"She told them she was Commodore Ireton's daughter when they were booking her," Tonelli said. "But the dumb desk sergeant wouldn't believe her. When we found the Commodore was dead, we put out a general alarm for her. The patrolman on her beat couldn't find her at the house, and the maid there told him she was at the Administration Building. We checked up there, found she had been there and gone. Meanwhile the alarm went through on the teletype to the stationhouse where she was being held with the gang. The sergeant read it and decided he better check up on the girl who said she was Commodore Ireton's daughter. He believed her the second time he talked to her. He called me, and I told him to put her in a squad car and send her up to the building. I guess you saw her there when she arrived," Tonelli said slyly.

"Yes," I said, "I saw her. So did Larry. He was with me and Graeme."

"Did he speak to Miss Ireton?" Tonelli asked.

"She didn't see me," said Larry. "I took care to keep out of her sight. I thought if she saw me then she might say or do something to betray us."

"Betray what?" Tonelli asked.

"Betray the fact that we knew each other. That's all we have to conceal," Larry answered steadily.

"So the Commodore didn't know anything about your knowing his daughter," Tonelli remarked. I've known the Lieutenant for a long while, and when he gets bland it's time for somebody to look out. There was trouble brewing for Mrs. Parsons' son Larry.

Larry tried to change the subject: "Is Jaze spending the night with her Aunt Margaret in Bellaire?" he asked.

Tonelli nodded yes.

"Listen, Larry," I said. "If the Commodore did know about you and his gal, and you had a brawl with him, you might as well spill. Sooner or later it's bound to come out."

Larry had lockjaw on the subject of the Commodore.

Tonelli got slowly to his feet. He gathered up his goods and chattels slowly, and said in his kindest tone:

"Well, I guess I gotta go now. It's too bad you have to spend the night in this place, but I guess you can fix it up with a bondsman in the morning. That is, unless the D.A. decides he wants to hold you as a material witness, in which event you may not be able to get bond. Is there any message you'd like me to take to the girl friend?"

Larry got red around the gills. "The best thing you can do for her," he growled, "is to let her alone. She's not getting much of a break, you know. It's not so easy, having your old man bumped off, even if you are—" He looked as if he had started to say something he shouldn't, and once again clamped his jaw.

I decided to play up to Tonelli. I said, "Listen, flatfoot, can't you do something for my pal here? You know he doesn't have to stay here all night. You can fix it if you want to."

Tonelli turned on all the juice. "I'd do anything in the world for you, you know, kid," he said to me, "and your friend here looks like a regular guy to me; but there's nothing I can do tonight."

I said, "Listen, Lieutenant, if you were to get some essential evidence out of Larry tonight, couldn't you strain a point and do something nice?"

"That," said Tonelli, "is a pony of another shade. S'posing I could get some dope, I might be able to pull a couple wires. I might be able," he added craftily, "to let on to the D.A.'s office that I turned the kid here loose and put a tail on him on account of how he knew such a lot and could lead us to something big."

I turned to Larry. "You're a playwright," I said. "There's the outline of your scenario. Why don't you fill it in? What do you care about a lie or two? It's better to lie than to sleep in one of those stinking cells."

"What's the difference?" said Larry. "I lie in a cell, and a turnkey watches me through the bars; or I lie to you here, and a sneaking copper follows me home watching me. I can't tell you anything."

Still playing up to Tonelli, "I've got a hunch," I said. "Maybe if we rush out to Bellaire and pull this Ireton dame out of bed and let on that Larry here has spilled a lot of stuff, we can get her to talk."

Larry was on his feet. He aimed a haymaker at my jaw, which missed because I jumped back—or maybe because Tonelli put his hand on Larry's chest and pushed. Anyway, the net result was that Larry swung across the room, smacked against the wall, slid down it to sit in a huddle and I found myself against the opposite wall.

"You rat," said Larry, both hands holding his head. It had smacked hard against the wall.

"That quick temper of yours," I told him sweetly, "is going to land you right in the hot seat. That's probably what you did to Commodore Ireton."

Tonelli was all the charming, reasonable cop once more. He said to me:

"Now what's the idea getting the boy all riled up?" and went over and lifted Larry to his feet. There we were back again, at the beginning. Larry was discouraged, glum, and in addition to being jail-nasty, he had lost any respect and confidence that he had in me. That in its way was all to the good. It was beginning to edge into his thoughts that Tonelli was his good friend. Tonelli was waiting for that shift, and began to work on him. He leaned over with a confidential manner and said:

"Now listen, kid. I saved you that time. I didn't want you to get your neck out. You're a prisoner now. You gotta be good. In the next few days there'll be a lot of people asking you a lot of questions. If you try to bop everybody who speaks rough to you, you're going to get plenty working over, and I don't mean maybe. Now look," said Tonelli, "I'm not trying to scare you or anything, but I just want to show you something."

He got Larry to stand up. With the heel of his hand he shoved Larry's left cheek up against the wall, so that Larry's face was sideways, with the end of his jawbone resting against the plaster. Then Tonelli put the heel of his hand against the other jawbone and leaned on it.

"Does that hurt, kid?" he asked.

"No," Larry mumbled, "but it could."

Tonelli leaned harder for just an instant, and relaxed the pressure before he hurt too much. He said:

"This is a trick some of these tough cops use. I'm not saying you'll get one of them questioning you, but you just might. He'll lean on your jawbone until you start talking. And if you don't start talking soon, your jawbone is going to crack, right at the point of your chin. It's a good stunt for the cops, because it doesn't leave any bruises and it can't be seen. But I'm telling you, it hurts."

I said, "Tonelli, you make me sick at my stomach." I guess I was about as white as Larry was. He rubbed his jaw, slumped back into the seat at the table.

"You can't intimidate me," he grumbled. That was kind of funny. I almost laughed out loud, because if Larry was not intimidated, they've got a new word for it.

I said, "Oh my God, Larry. Stop being a hero. It won't get you anywhere."

Larry said to me, "Shut up, rat."

Tonelli went through the motions again of getting ready to leave. "Don't say I didn't try to give you a break," he warned. He walked over to the door, opened it, and said to the turnkey outside: "All right, take him away."

Larry stood up with a dazed look in his eyes and moved toward the corridor. As he stepped outside of the room, the full flavor of that prison smell struck him. It lifted his head as though it had been jerked by a wire. He quivered all over and turned as gray as the dawn that was seeping in the window. He turned back, almost staggered to his chair, and buried his face in his arms.

"You win," he said. "I can't take it. I'll talk."

He talked steadily for an hour and a half, once he got started. He really didn't have a great deal to contribute. He and Jaze saw a lot of each other. They were trying to figure out a way of breaking the news to papa. Any way they figured it, they were in a spot. In the first place, Larry's WPA pay wasn't much to get married on; in the second place, the old man wouldn't take very kindly to the thought of his daughter marrying a man on work relief. In the third place, if Larry got cocky it would look as if he were putting the boots to the Commodore, bringing pressure to bear to get himself a better job. There were plenty of good jobs in WPA. Salaries ranging all the way up to the administrator's top, which was $15,000 per annum, or maybe it was $12,000. Anyway, it was plenty, from Larry's point of view, even if it was small potatoes to Morgan or U. S. Steel.

While the couple were seeing each other and debating, they wandered into a restaurant one night and there at a corner table, with his secretary Sarah Hirzner, sat WPA Administrator Commodore Henry H. Ireton. There were fireworks immediately, and conclusive. Ireton said his say, and it was plenty, delivered with punctuations of his fluid and peculiarly pungent profanity.

Sympathy goes to little Sarah Hirzner in that scene. The Commodore was sustained and elevated by his righteous indignation as a betrayed parent. Jaze and Larry were, of course, bolstered up by their equally virtuous and unassailable position as sincere and honest lovers. Poor little Hirzner was not only caught flatfooted, clandestinely dining with her boss, but she was not in the position of a major actor. All she could do was to shrink back and half hysterically go over and over her pitiful litany, "Please, Commodore, don't curse. Don't talk so loud. Please, Commodore, don't make a scene here; somebody may recognize you. Oh please, don't curse like that."

Larry said he let the old man have his head. He let the Commodore take the first two or three bites before he began to snap back. The Commodore told him off in the most approved fashion. He called him the standard names like snake-in-the-grass, creeping-destroyer-of-homes, degenerate, and the other playful little things fathers say to the worthless young men who have the temerity to fall in love with their daughters.

Larry, when it came his turn, pointed out that the Commodore was not exactly spotless. It might be that Larry was out with the Commodore's daughter without permission, but at least Larry was not a high-placed public official. He was not a family man. He was with honorable intent on a perfectly respectable expedition in search of food. The Commodore, on the contrary, was a lecherous old so-and-so who was using his official position to suborn the morals of a poor defenseless little gal whose job depended upon her smiling at the boss.

The girls then began to talk together, each saying almost the same thing. They both, in a breath, told Larry the Commodore was a widower and if he wanted to take a girl to dinner it was his business and the girl's business. Larry threw in parenthetically that her oleaginous tone when Sarah spoke of the Commodore was proof enough she was not there under duress. Larry marveled, also parenthetically, that anybody could be so close to that poisonous gila monster as Sarah had been, and still like him. But then, said Larry, Jaze liked him too; in fact, Larry continued, now that the Commodore was gone, he wouldn't be at all surprised if there wasn't something or other to be said in his favor. He didn't quite know what, but something.

Anyway, that restaurant encounter splashed the soup. The scene, if anything, had been all the more violent because the women precluded anything in the nature of fisticuffs. The verbal bout ended in a draw. Larry and Jaze left the place, but Larry got no dinner. Jaze insisted on going home immediately, by bus because, she insisted, Larry couldn't afford a taxi, which he couldn't.

"If I hadn't been so blind," said Larry sadly, "if I hadn't been so intent on Jaze, I would have recognized that official limousine outside the restaurant when we went in."

I said virtuously, "Why Larry. You don't mean to insinuate the Commodore used an official car on his own private and personal expeditions!"

Larry growled, "What do *you* think? There's a lot of those guys turning up mileage on official cars, and if you think it's all official business you've gone soft since you went on Government payroll."

From then on Larry was officially forbidden to see his beloved. The Commodore arranged for Jaze to be chaperoned day and night.

They beat that racket in the usual time-honored manner. Larry began to get telephone calls from Jaze's dearest girl friend. He began to call on Dearest Girl Friend, and strangely enough, whenever he called, Jaze happened to be dropping in and the friend would find other business to attend to while they talked and snuggled. The Commodore was nobody's fool. He knew this was going on, but Jaze was of age. She put it flatly to her father that if he got too tough she would simply walk out on him. That brought the Commodore to a semblance of reason, although it modified his language not a whit.

Larry began to find his life a burden. Up to this time he had been something of a white-haired boy on the job. It was true that he had taken a great interest in organization of the workers. He was the spearhead of an attack which had for its purpose more complete recognition of the rights and privileges of WPA workers. Larry was hopped up with an idea the program should be something more than work relief. He refused to accept for himself and his people the theory that he was a charge on the public purse, an object of charity being given a chance to work to maintain his self-respect only until he could get a job on the outside. He was all for government subsidization of art on a permanent basis. He had a good deal on his side, too.

But this bright-eyed idealist began to get his lumps. In the past if he had taken off a day or so to dash to Washington as the head of a delegation, the timekeeper was conveniently blind, or else the time was charged off to annual leave. Now he was docked for every minute he spent off the project during working hours. That's a little hard to take, for a playwright or a play producer works from the time he gets up till the time he goes to bed, if he is of the right stuff—which Larry was. Why should such a worker punch a time clock? He can, and does, work anywhere.

Larry ventured to ask some of his superiors if word had been passed down from the Commodore's office to make his life a burden.

This was politely and smilingly denied, but petty persecution continued. The next step was to bring Larry on the carpet. No matter what he did, it was wrong. He broke more regulations than he knew existed. He actually hadn't a chance, because the WPA rule book contains the usual governmental brain teasers plus a lot of new ones ingenious braintrusters and inquisitorial social workers have thought up on their own hook. Treasury officials examined his accounts with a microscope. If he put through a requisition, the Department of Procurement or Equipment and Supplies found it was made out wrong and was against the law.

Larry was fit to be tied. His mood communicated itself to Jaze. Every time they saw each other they ended in a drawn battle over the Commodore and his methods. Larry knew the Commodore's own private secret service, his personal OGPU, was watching him. It got so Larry didn't dare go to a Project Council meeting, or to a meeting of the unions: His fellow project workers couldn't understand the situation. They figured Larry was selling out, backing out, getting cold feet, had ceased to be the peerless leader he once had seemed. Life closed in on Larry.

At this juncture he sought, and obtained, another interview with the Commodore. The Commodore offered to send him out to the West Coast. He offered to get him a job on a newspaper. He offered him a trip around the world. He offered almost everything—except what a decent, self-respecting man could accept; and when Larry turned down all the offers, they went at it again, calling each other names, until the Commodore frothed at the mouth and Sarah, chanting her refrain of "Please stop cursing," came in and put Larry out.

"And yet," said Tonelli thoughtfully, "you were the leader of that gang waiting to protest against cuts in the projects, weren't you?"

Larry admitted that. His point was that he couldn't lay down on his pals. He had gone so far with them that now there was no turning back. He made some speech about the Commodore being a rational man, and not allowing his private personal affairs to obscure his judgment as Administrator. I laughed a lot at that. Larry was too warm, and Tonelli was too intent on being sympathetic, to join in.

"So when you got a chance, you slipped in the Commodore's office and strangled him," said Tonelli, quite as if he were saying, "so you went in and had a cup of tea."

Equally unemotionally Larry said, "Nuts, Lieutenant. You know that isn't so."

Now that he was worn down to a nub, Larry was far more convincing than when he was on his high horse.

"Will Miss Ireton and Miss Hirzner back up what you've told me?" asked Tonelli.

"I don't know what Sarah will say," Larry maintained stoutly, "but Jaze will tell the truth. Exactly as I've told you."

"Have you any reason to believe that Miss Ireton did not like her father as much as she pretended to?" Tonelli asked.

Larry looked at him sharply. "Why do you ask that?"

"No reason," said Tonelli, "except that quite a while back you began some statement in regard to Miss Ireton's feeling toward her father. You caught yourself before you committed yourself to anything. Do you remember?"

Larry shook his head. "I don't remember anything like that."

"It was probably just a slip of the tongue," said Tonelli easily.

I watched the lieutenant. As I said before, when the oil began dripping from Tonelli it was time to watch the brute. I didn't know Jaze then, but I had great confidence in Larry's judgment. If he had fallen for a jane, she was something to fall for; and my sympathies are always with young and beautiful gals. At least theoretically. I'm willing to believe them guilty until they're proven innocent, or vice versa.

There was a long silence. I finished up a package of cigarettes, balled the paper into a wad and tried to throw it between the bars of the window.

Tonelli growled at me, "What's the idea? Do you want some yard guard cutting loose with a submachine gun?"

I told him, "No, thanks," besides I hadn't anything further to throw. I asked him what he was going to do about Larry, now that he had his story. Tonelli considered. Finally he said:

"Will you promise to go straight home, to stay there, to talk to nobody, not even on the telephone, and to be ready any time you're called to answer questions the police or the D.A. wants to put to you?"

Larry thought it would be nice if he could call up Jaze just once. Tonelli would have none of it, and Larry finally agreed. It took a couple of hours and all the pull Tonelli had, to spring the lad; but finally the deed was done and I rode him home in a taxi. When I got back to my hotel it was too late to go to bed. I had a shower, and my breakfast sent up to my room. In the midst of my second slice of toast—yes, you've guessed it—the telephone buzzed. It was Tonelli.

"I thought so," he said triumphantly. "The first move that mug made as soon as he got home was to call up his gal. I had my men on the wire. He warned her to tell nobody nothing. Now what can you do for a dumb mug like that?"

"Throw him back in the can," I advised. "It might be a break for him at that. If you let him alone, he'll marry the woman."

"You've got a terrible down on the Ireton dame," Tonelli said. "What'd she ever do to you?"

"I made a pass at her once," I told him, "and it was no dice."

5

IZZIE WAS ON THE JOB bright and early the next morning. I went up to the Administration Building at nine o'clock and wangled a desk and chair for myself. In order to do it, I had to convince a couple of dozen supernumeraries that I actually was from Washington and did rate a parking place. Izzie appeared while I was arguing with them, and made everything doubly difficult by being officiously helpful. His technique was wonderful. He halted every guard we passed, ordered the man to look me over, and to remember me "because," Izzie would say impressively, "Mr. Moore is a very busy man, and I shouldn't want for any of the guards to hold him up and waste none of his time."

He was so helpful that when he invited me to go to the hospital with him to see Bennington Graeme, I went, just to keep him from smothering me with attention.

Benny looked pretty chipper for a dead man. The nurse told me his injuries had been a little exaggerated in Izzie's first reports. The X-rays had come through, and except for a broken rib he was in pretty fair shape. He was not inclined to talk about his experience.

I asked him if he knew who had done the dastardly deed, and he denied he knew anything about men or motives.

"I left the party a few minutes after you did," he said. "I was walking down the street when a car drove up. A man leaned out of the car and said, 'Get in, we'll drive you home.' I thought it was somebody who'd been at the party, and I got in. Immediately one of two men in the back seat hit me. He didn't knock me out, and I struggled. Then he hit me again, and then I suppose one of them struck me with something like a blackjack or a sandbag, because I don't remember any more until I came to in the water. In the river. I'm a pretty good swimmer, and I suppose that's what saved me. I managed to yell for help, and hang on to the piling of the dock until somebody on the pierhead crawled down, looped a rope around me, and pulled me back."

Izzie said very bright-eyed and seriously, "Have you got any secret enemies, Mr. Graeme?"

Benny snorted. "Enemies!" he said. "Of course I've got enemies. Nobody can work on this job and not have enemies. Every time I hire somebody or fire somebody or raise somebody's pay or demote somebody, I make a dozen enemies."

Izzie shook his head wisely. "Then that's it," he said. "You know any man that holds public office, Mr. Graeme, is always in danger."

"Maybe Mr. Graeme is too weak to talk," I suggested to Izzie. Izzie said, "Certainly, certainly, we wouldn't bother you, Mr. Graeme—but if you just could remember one little tiny thing about the persons that assaulted you—"

"I can remember one great big thing," Benny said grimly. "And that is the size of the guy's fist who hit me when I first stepped into that limousine."

"Now there is something," Izzie seized on this eagerly. "It was a man with a big fist, and it was a limousine."

"Not exactly a limousine, maybe," said Graeme, "but it was a large closed car very much like these cars the WPA uses."

Izzie's eyes got as big as saucers. "You wouldn't think maybe it *was* a WPA car?" he asked hopefully.

Pulling him away, I said scornfully, "Have we got an assault-and-battery project now?"

"You're always kidding, ain't you, Mr. Moore," said Izzie admiringly.

I called back to Bennington Graeme, "I'll send you a bunch of daisies as soon as I get my expense money."

Benny said, "Save it. Buy me a couple of Clover Clubs after I get out."

Back at the office I called up the Arts directors one by one and made appointments with them. The first was with Mrs. Flood for luncheon.

At a quarter to one I turned up at the Federal Theatre head-quarters. Mrs. Flood's office was something like a railroad station just before the 5:15 pulls out. People rushed in, whispered things in her ear; the telephone rang constantly; and there was the inevitable delegation waiting in the outside office. They were from the dancers. The dancers didn't like their director, and he reciprocated. The director told his story, and the dancers told their story. It was the same story: each said the other was lousy. The dance director couldn't direct; the dancers couldn't dance.

Meanwhile I got hungrier and hungrier, but Mrs. Flood went serenely on. She talked to Washington, she talked to the head of the Experimental Theatre, she argued with the Vaudeville Unit, the Suitcase Theatre was having trouble with its bookings, the Workshop couldn't turn out scenery fast enough for the Yiddish Players. Everybody was excited, everybody was intense. Commodore Ireton's murder seemed so inconsequential by the time we did get to lunch that Mrs. Flood's first question took me by surprise.

"Who do you think murdered Commodore Ireton?" she asked.

"Probably you," I said. "You've forgotten it. How could you remember a murder, with all you've got on your mind?"

She peered at me across the table, decided it was a joke, and smiled weakly. She ordered clam broth, a pear salad, with cream cheese, and coffee. I ordered everything on the table d'hote. I don't know how she did it. Three-quarters of an hour's sitting in her office had worn me out, but she kept it up day after day, twelve hours at a stretch, on bird rations, and never drank a drop.

We got down to a heavy analysis of the events leading up to the tragedy. It was a little difficult to think of it as a tragedy. These people were human, sympathetic, very much interested in the welfare and comfort of their fellow beings; but for some reason or other there was no horror that Commodore Ireton was dead. The sight of the dead man the day before had made me ill, but as soon as that actual physical spasm had passed I found myself disgustingly calm.

In my own case it was perhaps not so strange, because I had not known the Commodore well or intimately. My one encounter with him had been violent, but I felt no kinship to him. Men I have hated, and with whom I have quarreled usually leave me with as intense a personal interest as friends would. I follow their ups and downs eagerly. But the Commodore left no personal spark. The Commodore was just a number to me, and while nobody else said just that, they acted that way too.

With salt cellars and diagrams scraped on the tablecloth with the tines of a fork, Mrs. Flood and I attempted to reconstruct the crime. I had hoped for a lot of help from her. Being a woman of the theatre, used to visualizing stage sets, and grouping and arranging people, it was reasonable to suppose she had the rudiments of a camera eye. The tablecloth proving inadequate, I tore a page out of a notebook and we tried to draw the interior plan of Commodore Ireton's office, and to place the people in their positions in the Conference Room as we remembered them. It was no go.

The best that happened was that Mrs. Flood, in trying to work it all out, practically proved herself to have been the last person to leave the conference room.

"You know," she said, "I distinctly recall—or I think I recall—that as I went to the door I stopped and looked back toward the Commodore. My impulse was to say, 'Aren't you coming?'"

"Don't you recall seeing anybody with or near the Commodore?" I asked her.

She was doubtful, but after a while said, "No, I didn't see anybody."

"What did you do when you got outside the office?" I asked.

"I wanted to run back in again," she told me, "but I didn't. I stood out there, just outside the door of the conference room, trying to press myself into the wooden panel of the partition, and watched and tried not to scream."

"If you wanted to go back in, why didn't you?" I asked.

"I don't know," she confessed. "Except that I have a feeling we are responsible for these people. Their troubles are our troubles, and when they are in trouble we should share with them or at least stand by."

"How strong *is* that conviction of yours?" I asked.

"Just what do you mean?" she countered.

"If you actually feel this way, would you be willing to take a chance on your own life and security to help the people who are working on your program?"

"I believe I would, if it came right down to it," she said quietly.

"Then," I drew the inference, "it is not beyond the bounds of possibility that if you felt Commodore Ireton to be a menace to the security of the workers on your project, or of the project itself, you wouldn't hesitate to eliminate Commodore Ireton."

"No," she said quite as quietly as before, "I would not hesitate, if I actually thought that Commodore Ireton had been a menace to my people or to my project."

"Do you know what a statement you're making?" I demanded.

"Yes, I do," she acknowledged. "And I make it because I am sure you know or feel that I did not kill Commodore Ireton, and that even if you suspected it you would not tell the police."

How she knew that is beyond me. As a matter of fact, when I had invited her to lunch I had every intention of pumping her and turning over any valuable information I might get to Tonelli. That sojourn in her office may have changed me. One couldn't stay around Mrs. Flood for any length of time without being imbued with something of her spirit. She was both magnetic and dynamic. She had absolutely no executive ability. Her approach to the theatre was not so much emotional as sentimental. She was full of the wrong kind of reactions to the right kind of things. She was a contradiction, a person without the flair to lead, but she shone like a lamp in the darkness in spite of it. She wanted so damn much for the Federal Theatre to be a great success, she practically wished it across the line.

To suspect her of murder was easy. To believe she was a murderess was beyond my imagination. To turn her in as a suspect was impossible.

"Mrs. Flood," I asked her, "did you have any particular thing that you intended taking up with Commodore Ireton at that conference yesterday?"

She hesitated so long in replying I was sure she didn't want to answer. Finally she said, "Yes."

I waited.

"One thing I had made up my mind to say to him," she began. "It was something that might be misconstrued, and that I wouldn't have the police know for anything. Some time back, Commodore Ireton asked me to come to see him. I went. And he asked me to recommend the dismissal of one of the people working with me."

"Who was that?" I asked.

"Larry Parsons. I asked the Commodore upon what possible grounds I could discharge him. He fell into a terrific rage. He told me that it was not for me to ask questions, but to obey orders. I told him I felt it was distinctly my duty to ask questions about any matter that affected the welfare of my project. I said it seemed to me as long as Larry's play was in rehearsal he should be permitted to continue on the payroll. He was a good workman and there was no cause for his dismissal."

"What did the old geezer say to that?" I demanded.

"He said," she told me, "he had reason to believe Larry was a bad influence. He was a troublemaker. He kept everybody stirred up, and he, the Commodore, was determined to get rid of Larry."

"You stuck to your guns?" I asked.

"I did; but I was not quite sure of my ground," she admitted. "It would be hard to defend Larry's actions under ordinary conditions. Larry *has* been an agitator. He believes, as many of us do, that there should be a permanent theatre."

I shook my head.

"Oh yes," she answered my gesture, "you're from Washington. You have the official attitude. This is a work program to you. You think our dreams of a subsidized art movement are impractical. But—we still have those dreams. And some day you will have to acknowledge we were right."

"Did it occur to you," I asked her, "that the Commodore's interest in Larry was more personal than a mere dislike for an agitator?"

She cocked her head wisely.

"How much do you know?" she asked me.

"Plenty," I said.

"And you want to find out how much I know," she said. "I don't mind. I'll tell you. I know Larry has been seeing the Commodore's daughter. These projects, you know, are regular sounding boards. Everything that goes on is seen, snatched up, repeated, magnified, and distorted. We directors get back stories of our personal lives that would be tragic and alarming if they were not so palpably amusing."

"Then," I said, "if Larry thought he was conducting a quiet little courtship, he was way off the track."

She laughed. "Way, way off the track. Why, everybody in the projects has been hanging on his every action. He is the romantic interest in the lives of hundreds of WPA workers. They're pulling for him. They want him to marry the girl."

"Do you think," I asked her, "Larry is capable of bumping off the Commodore?"

She looked frightened at that. She took a long time to answer, and when she did she was very indirect. She said:

"I think Larry is a dear, sweet boy, and I think he is very desperate. Very much in love."

"Then you think he might have done it?" I put it to her.

"I have no business to say anything of the sort," she parried my question. She rose and began to struggle with her coat.

THREE THINGS WERE WAITING for me at the Administration Building when I got there. The first was a telegram from Washington; the second was a message to call Benjamin Cook as soon as I got in; and the third was Lieutenant Pietro Tonelli. Tonelli had spent his time during my absence in going over the Commodore's office, the scene of the murder. He was sitting at my temporary desk, smoking a large cigar, when I got there.

The telegram read:

BY ORDER ADMINISTRATOR WORKS PROGRESS ADMINISTRATION YOU ARE TO TAKE CHARGE OF ALL ACTIVITIES IN YOUR PRESENT DISTRICT WITH TITLE OF ACTING DEPUTY ADMINISTRA- TOR STOP MAYOR AND OTHER NECESSARY AUTHORITIES ARE BEING ADVISED SIMULTA- NEOUSLY WITH YOUR RECEIPT OF THIS AUTHO- RIZATION

BENJAMIN COOK

I immediately grabbed the phone, put in a call for Ben, and got him at once.

"Now don't go crazy," Ben said. "The only reason we put you in charge was because there wasn't anybody else we could trust. Don't disturb anything. Don't hire anybody, and don't fire anybody. Just keep everything as nearly on an even keel as you can, and don't make any decisions that will have to be unmade later."

"In other words," I said, "I'm just to sit."

"If you can sit and get away with it, that's swell," said Ben. "It's the hardest job in the world, though. Remember anything you do is likely to be wrong. And by the way, one thing is very important: get hold of all of the files, confidential reports, and correspondence, everything in Commodore Ireton's personal files, and sit on them until we can get somebody to take charge and to act on things that require action."

I said, "How long am I going to enjoy this exalted position?"

"I don't know," said Ben. "Maybe twenty-four hours, maybe a week. Just sit."

"How much raise of pay goes with it?" I demanded.

Ben said, "Nuts."

Tonelli was grinning broadly when I hung up. "Well," he said.

"You are looking," I boasted, "at the new Acting Deputy Administrator of this district."

Pete said seriously, "Congratulations. I'm glad it's you. I know where I stand with you, and I can work with you."

"All right," I said. "As my first official action I want a report on your progress so far. Have you got any line on who murdered the Commodore?"

"I been walking over the ground again this morning while I was waiting for you," said Pete. "Come over to the Commodore's office, and I'll show you what I mean."

The Commodore's office was locked, and guarded by two uniformed policemen. In the regular routing, everything had been left exactly as it was at the time of the murder—except the corpse. Even though it was a murder room, it looked very cheerful this afternoon. The sun was streaming in the windows, and lit up the piles of reports and manuscript on the desk, which was the dominant object in the room. In point of fact, there was a desk and a table, between which the Administrator sat. There were ten or twelve chairs, and the bookshelves which had sheltered my shame the day before. Pete walked over to the desk and sat in the chair.

"Now I'm the Commodore," he said, "and you're the murderer. Now you are just coming through the door—"

"Which door?" I asked.

"All right, all right," said Pete. "I'm not trying to trap you into anything. Just start over there in the corner between the two doors. We don't know which door you came in. You might have come in the door from the outside, and you might have come through the secretary's room. Both doors were unlocked, and it's a cinch you came through one of them."

I said, "I don't like all this insistence on 'you.'"

Pete made a growling noise. I stepped over in the vicinity of the two doors, and started walking in the direction of the desk.

Pete said, "Hello. What are you doing here?"

I stopped in front of the desk and said, "Playing cops and robbers, and making a damn fool out of myself."

A big smile lighted up Pete's face. "You see!" he said.

"See what?" I demanded.

"Why, see where you stopped," said Pete. "You stopped right in front of the desk."

This thing was getting on my nerves.

I said, "Where the hell did you expect me to stop—on the window sill?"

"Use your head," said Pete. "This is what I'm getting at: the guy that killed Commodore Ireton was behind him."

I said, "Yeah."

"Now," Pete went on, "suppose you knew the Commodore pretty well. Suppose you were on good terms with him. Suppose you were an old buddy of his."

"Don't be silly," I said. "I choose my friends."

"All right, crack wise," he said. "But you see what I mean. If you were a good friend of the Commodore's, you wouldn't stop in front of the desk necessarily. You'd pass around the side of the desk. You'd stand right here," he pointed to a spot a little to his left and slightly behind him. "Suppose you were leaning over his shoulder, showing him something, like this."

He picked up one of the reports from the desk, swung around until he was facing it, and held the report in his two hands as if he

were reading it. I stepped to his side and went through the pan-
tomime he suggested. I leaned partly across him, and pointed to
something in the report. At my feet was a wastepaper basket, still as
it had been the previous day. In the wastepaper basket were wrap-
pings, crumpled papers, and several long strands of cord, which the
Commodore had snipped from the bundles of reports that he was
reading.

As I leaned over with my right hand pointing, my left hand hanging at my side, the tips of my left fingers were within a few inches of
that cord in the wastebasket.

"Hold that position," said Pete. "Look where your left hand is.
You could pick up a piece of that cord very quickly, couldn't you?"

"Yes," I said.

"And the Commodore," said Pete, "is leaning over the desk. Now
all you got to do is grab a piece of that cord with your left hand. Your
right hand is almost in position. You whip the cord around the Commodore's neck, and there you are!"

"Yes," I said, "and the Commodore screams bloody murder, and
nineteen guards and his secretary come busting in here."

"You haven't seen the medical report," said Pete sadly. "According to the docs, it didn't take much to bump off Commodore Ireton. He was almost dead anyhow. He had a bum heart, and his liver
was bad. When they opened him up at the autopsy he had just about
everything possible wrong with his works. He would have died
almost before you began putting the pressure on him."

"Pete," I said, "just as a favor, will you stop saying *I* did this?"

"In a minute," said Pete, "I'll begin to believe you *did* do it, if you
don't stop squawking."

"So, with all this reconstruction," I demanded, "what have you
got? It sounds reasonable to me. This is the way the murder was
committed, I have no doubt. But it doesn't help you a bit as to who
killed the Commodore, nor why."

"No," said Pete gloomily, "it does leave us pretty much where we
started. Only this, now, we do know: whoever killed the Commodore
was kind of palsy-walsy with him. Somebody he knew well."

"Izzie!" I said. "He fits in swell. One of Izzie's favorite gestures is
to lean over you and blow secrets and onions in your ear."

"Naah," said Tonelli, "it wasn't that mug. I kinda wish it was, but he didn't do it. You see, what you say about the Commodore yelling for help has something to it. This murder was committed while the riot was at its height out there. It was done when everybody was yelling. The person that did it wasn't taking no chance at all. The Commodore might have yelled, but nobody heard him. Everybody was too busy doing something else. In fact, your friend Izzie was right with me most of the time, and yelling as loud as anybody else. So that kinda lets him out."

"Danny Mulroy came in here," I said. "Sometimes the Commodore made him mad enough to commit murder. Why don't you ask him?"

"They'll all be on the grill this afternoon and tomorrow," said Pete. "I'm watching 'em, and I'll put 'em over the jumps."

"What about this famous technical staff of yours?" I asked him. "What about this new process they say will bring out fingerprints on anything? Have you tested that rope for fingerprints?"

Pete snorted. "Be your age," he said. "You know all them fancy doodads are no good when you really need 'em. You've been a press agent, and a newspaper guy. You know all that stuff's just a build-up for the G-men."

"By the way, when do Hoover's boys arrive?" I asked.

Pete looked annoyed. "This is no federal case. Done right here in town. Murder's not a federal offense, unless it breaks some federal law while it's being done."

"They'll find a way," I soothed him. "Just about when you've got this thing all cleared up, Dick Tracy will come galumphing in and eat up all the marmalade."

Pete changed the subject.

"Did Miss Sarah Hirzner come in to work this morning?" he asked.

I grinned at him. "You tell me," I said. "You've probably got one of your dicks sleeping with her, by now."

"No," said Pete seriously, "she's not that kind of a girl. She's pretty well shot over the death of the Commodore. We're not keeping a close watch on her. I have a man over there, but she hasn't stirred out of the house today. The doctor's been there. He says she's suffering from nervous shock and won't be able to get up out of bed for four-five days."

"That's nice," I said. "Just when I need her. She's probably the only person around here that knows anything about the Commodore's confidential and official papers. I've had orders to get hold of those papers, and I don't see how I'm going to do it without her."

Tonelli's face lit up. "Say," he said, "that's an idea. That gives me an excuse for going to see her without getting her all worked up. Come along, take me over to her house. She's got a little flat over on the South side."

"Do your own dirty work," I snapped.

"Look here," said Pete, "you're the boss man around here now, and you've got to work with the police. Come on, get your hat and coat. We're going over to see Sarah Hirzner."

"I've got work to do, Pete," I protested. "I'm the new Administrator."

"All right," said Pete, "what have you got to do?"

He had me there. I got my hat and coat.

6

THERE WAS NONE of this screaming-siren business about Pete Tonelli. We got into his car, an ordinary touring car to outward appearances, and drove sedately, obeying all traffic lights, to Sarah Hirzner's apartment. A plainclothesman lounging across the street from the apartment came to the curb to report.

"Everything okay?" Pete asked.

"Sure," said the plainclothesman. "Nothing happened at all."

"You've been here all morning?" Pete asked.

"Well, I been moving around a little bit," the detective said. "And at noontime I went down the street and got me a cup of coffee. I got an in with the elevator boys. They would've told me if anybody came in while I was gone."

Pete nodded. We left the car across the street and walked over to the apartment.

"I've got the telephone wire covered," Pete told me. "Nobody could call in or out of the apartment without my knowing it."

The eight-story apartment building was built around a central court. Sarah Hirzner's apartment was on the second floor, in the front. A nice place; the kid had done all right for herself.

We went up in the elevator, and as we got off Pete indicated an exit door right next to Sarah Hirzner's apartment.

"A good layout," observed Pete. "Just right for a gal having a gent call on her which she didn't want anybody to know about it. You could slip in and out of the basement and up the stairs through this fire door here, and nobody would ever see you in the front of the house. I guess that's the way the Commodore used to come in and out. I'll have to move my man from across the street. All he can see there is the front door."

He rang the doorbell, and we had a long wait. He rang again, a second and a third time, and still there was no response.

Pete tried the door, but it was locked.

I said, "Hasn't she got a maid?"

"No," said Pete. "She didn't have a nurse, either. The doc didn't think she was bad enough off for that; all she needed was a rest."

I said, "I guess she got tired of waiting for you to come to see her, and went out for a walk."

"We'll see about that," Pete said threateningly. He pulled a bunch of skeleton keys from his hip pocket. "You run downstairs and get the superintendent," he ordered. "I'll try to get this door open in the meantime."

It took me a few minutes to locate the superintendent, but he finally came with his pass key. The outside door was open, and Pete was in the apartment. With the superintendent, I started in. Pete was at the telephone.

"And get the ambulance here right away," he finished a report he was making.

He looked at me, and I looked at him. He jerked his head in the direction of the front of the apartment.

"She's here," he said, "come along."

The three-room apartment had a large living room, kitchenette, bath, and a bedroom. Both bedroom and living room were at the front, and all the rooms opened off a small square foyer. It was nicely but not expensively furnished, comfortable and homelike, with good taste on the department store level.

Pete led the way into the bedroom, me on his heels and the superintendent gawping over our shoulders. Sarah Hirzner was in the bed. The shades had been snapped up to the top, and in the strong light the room looked disheveled, vaguely bawdy, as any tumbled bedroom does in the middle of the afternoon.

Pete bent over the girl. "See this?" he said.

There was a splotch of blood on the pillowcase. She was breathing deeply, stertorously, with rattling inspirations. Pete turned her head gently on the pillow, and explored at the base of the skull with unusually tender fingers.

"Mush," he said. "Somebody socked her a dirty whack."

"Is she dying?" I asked.

"I think so," said Pete. He straightened up and looked around the room. Backed away from the bed and lifted the trailing bedclothes to see under it. He stooped to pick up a heavy bronze ornament. An incense burner. One of those gadgets women keep on bedside tables to get knocked over in the dark. Pete, handling it as carefully as if it were rare Satsuma ware, examined the surface closely. At much greater distance from it than he, I could see blood and humus and a hair or two stuck to it.

Pete nodded. "That's it," he said. "That's the thing that did the business." He wrapped his handkerchief carefully around the thing, and put it in his pocket.

"Will your experts find fingerprints on that?" I asked.

"They ought," said Pete, "but I got a hunch they won't."

"How come your plainclothesman didn't see or hear anybody coming in here?" I asked him.

Pete growled, "Just between you and me, that louse is going to be in the breadline this time next week. Him and his cup of coffee," he muttered disgustedly.

On the bed Sarah Hirzner stirred uneasily and we both turned to her. Her lips were dry, moving feebly as if she were trying to say something.

"Get me a glass of water out of the bathroom," Pete ordered.

I got it, and Pete carefully moistened her lips with a little of the water. It had no effect. Her breathing continued deep and irregular and rasping.

At the clangor of a bell in the street outside, I stepped to the window to watch the ambulance drive up. The usual brash and cocky young interne with his shabby overcoat over immaculate white, his battered blue peaked cap and his inevitable black bag came bounding along the court as if he were on his way to a picnic. Pete said to the superintendent, "See that the doctor gets in here right away." But the doctor was at the door before the superintendent could get through the foyer.

He came bustling in, flipping his hand in greeting in Tonelli's direction.

"Hiya, Lieutenant," he said, and went immediately to the bed.

On his heels came the plainclothesman Pete had left to watch the place. He was a very sick looking dick.

Tonelli bent over the bed with the doctor.

"What about it?" he asked.

The interne's face had lost all of its holiday freshness.

"Bad concussion," he diagnosed. "Brain affected."

"She's dying," stated Pete.

"Yes," said the doctor.

"Any chance of her regaining consciousness?" Tonelli asked.

The doctor shook his head. "It's doubtful," he said. "But there's always a chance."

"How about moving her?" Pete asked. "Are you going to take her to the hospital?"

"We'd better," the doctor decided. "There's one chance in several million that she might pull through, and we may as well take that chance."

"I'll ride in the ambulance with you," Pete decided. "You," he turned on his plainclothesman, "park your flat feet right inside this door. I'm going to send a real man up here as soon as I can get him, but in the meantime don't let anybody in this apartment, and don't let anybody touch anything."

"Yes, sir," the dick said humbly.

They took the stretcher down in the elevator and out the front door. I tagged along. I expected Pete at any moment to shoo me away, but he didn't. The interne seemed to think I was a member of the Police Department, and I didn't disillusion him. They slid the stretcher into the rack, and the interne crawled in and sat at the dying girl's head. Pete came in next, and I brought up the rear. We clanged along with the interne working all the while. Nothing happened. Sarah Hirzner lay there and labored with her snoring, pitiful breath.

At the hospital Pete and I followed right along through the receiving room into the special room they had assigned her, and stood by while the house surgeon made his examination and diagnosis.

He too shook his head.

"Not a chance," he told Pete. "She's gone. She may lie like this for an hour, or even longer, but there's nothing can be done for her."

Once again Pete asked wistfully, "Isn't there any possibility that she may come to for just a minute? Just long enough to answer one question. Just long enough to hint once who did it?"

The house surgeon shrugged his shoulders.

"It's just possible," he admitted. "We can try."

"Don't do anything to hurt the poor kid," Tonelli said. "But if she's dying anyway, and there's any possibility of getting anything out of her, she might rest easier in her grave if she knew we were on the track of the guy that done it."

While the doctors and a couple of nurses fussed around with oxygen tanks and bandages and antiseptics, I walked over and looked out of the window. At least I tried to look out of the window, but I kept stealing glances at what was going on at the bedside, and I was very glad when one of the nurses put up the screen so that I could see nothing.

It was evidently too much for Tonelli too. He came over and stood near me, but facing the bed, with his ears cocked for the faintest sound from the girl or for word or signal from the doctor. The doctor finished, the nurses rolled out the dressing wagon, and took away the screen; and when I looked again Sarah Hirzner's head was a great white blob of bandages. A nurse stayed beside her, and Tonelli went and stood by the nurse.

Someone came to the door to summon the house doctor, who went out saying to Tonelli as he left:

"That's about all we can do. She may stir, she may come to for a flash, she may go into delirium just before she dies, she may do nothing except stop breathing. It's the best we can do for you."

"Okay," said Pete. "Thank you, doctor. I'll stick right here by her as long as there's a ghost of a chance."

"What about me?" I asked. "You don't need my help, do you, Pete?"

"You better stay," Pete ordered. "If she did come to, she might say something you'd be interested in."

"Well, this is one murder you can't accuse me of," I cracked, my nerves on edge. "I've got a perfect alibi for all day today."

Pete snapped his fingers. "Jeest," he said, "I was so sorry for the poor kid I forgot all about asking the doc what time she was hit. Miss," he said to the nurse, "could you get hold of that doctor and ask him what time he thinks this happened?"

The girl went to the door, summoned a passing probationer, and sent her off on Tonelli's errand. In a few minutes the answer came back.

"The doctor says that as nearly as he can figure it out, the young lady was struck sometime between 12:30 and 1:30 this afternoon."

Suddenly the nurse sitting at the head of the bed was on her feet, attentive and eager. Sarah Hirzner's head rolled weakly from side to side, her lips parted again in that feeble gesture of speech. The nurse leaned over and moistened her lips. Faint sounds began to come from the dying woman's throat. Pete, on the opposite side of the bed from the nurse, leaned far over, his ear close to the dying girl's mouth. It was not necessary. She began to speak quite audibly. She whimpered at first, like a child who's being beaten, and then fragments of words began to come.

"No, no . . . Henry— No, not that— Swearing— No —"

The faint voice trailed away again. Tonelli looked desperately at the nurse. She took some smelling salts from the table and passed them once across under Sarah's nostrils. There was no immediate response, but soon again the feeble rolling of the head began, again incoherent mutterings, and then quite clearly and sharply:

"No! Don't do that! Stop it . . . Oh, the Commodore's—terrible— Commodore's cussin'—"

I gritted my teeth. I'd only seen Sarah Hirzner the day before, once or twice, and every time I'd seen her she had been in a panic over Commodore Ireton's frightful blasphemy and swearing. And here she was, dying, still worried over the Commodore's profanity, even in delirium.

The muttering had ceased. The nurse leaned over sharply, stood erect, and pressed a call button. She looked at Tonelli and then at me.

"It's all over," she said.

Completely in silence, Tonelli and I left the hospital and got a taxi to ferry us back to Sarah Hirzner's apartment. Tonelli's car was still parked opposite the building, and I got one laugh out of the day when I saw a ticket for overtime parking attached to its wheel. Tonelli didn't think it was funny.

The dick he had left guarding the place was very much on the alert now, and pea-green with anxiety over the grilling he knew he was bound to get. With scant preliminaries, Tonelli started in on him.

The Lieutenant ensconced himself in the easiest chair in the living room, a man's chair in brown leather, with ashtray and smoking kit within easy reaching distance. Undoubtedly the Commodore's favorite seat, that chair had been.

"Now, heel," Tonelli began, "let's hear what you've got to say for yourself. Start in from the beginning of your tour of duty this morning, and by God if you forget any detail or hold back anything I'll not only have you broke but jailed."

The man standing stiffly at attention began to talk in the curious clipped lingo policemen always use in giving testimony. They would rather say "premises" than "house" any day, and they're always "proceeding" somewhere. This fellow said:

"I reported for duty at 7 A. M. and took up my post opposite the premises. My instructions was to watch for any person or persons that might enter or leave this building, particularly those who entered or left the domicile of Miss Sarah Hirzner."

Tonelli exploded, "For God's sake sit down and talk like a human being. You ain't in magistrate's court now."

The man breathed a long sigh of relief and sat.

"Like I said, Lieutenant, I took up this job this morning and the first thing I did was to come over and make myself right with the elevator boys and the hallboy. They got two boys running the elevators during the rush times, and one boy on the door. He handles the switchboard too. From about 7:30 to a quarter of nine there was a lot of people going out. I stood around in the hall near the door-boy but he identified them all as tenants in the building. Then there wasn't so many, until about quarter of ten, and after that nobody come out but people walking dogs and a couple nursemaids with kids. About 10: 10 Miss Hirzner's doctor called. He went up to see her and I seen him when he come out. He said she was all right but that she needed rest from excitement."

"Wasn't there any maid going into the apartment? Didn't any-body collect the garbage or trash?" Tonelli demanded.

"No, sir. The hall boys told me Miss Hirzner had a maid in twice a week to do the heavy cleaning and the laundry. She cleaned up for herself between times. She didn't eat in the place much. She fixed her own breakfast, but she always had her lunch downtown and usually she was out for dinner. The grocer didn't deliver much. She usually stopped by and brought her own butter and eggs with her of an evening."

"How about her breakfast this morning?" Tonelli asked.

"She had that sent in from the corner drug store. I seen the boy that brought it, and he's the same boy that works behind the fountain."

Tonelli nodded. "Okay. Go on."

"After the doctor left—it musta been about eleven o'clock—the downstairs man collected the trash. One of the elevator boys went off duty at half past ten and don't come back to work till half past four. The boys take turn and turnabout on a short day."

"What about the entrance through the basement?" Tonelli asked. "You knew about that, I suppose?"

The man shifted uneasily in his chair. "Yes, sir, I knew about it. But in order to get in that way you have to go through the laundry and right past the furnace room. The superintendent or the furnace man is down there all the time, and they promised to tip me off if they seen anybody."

Tonelli got sarcastic. "Looks to me like you might as well've gone home and had a little nap. You had the elevator boys and the door-man watching the front, and the superintendent and a furnace man watching the back."

"Well," the man was somewhat aggrieved, "I ain't but one man, Lieutenant. I couldn't watch both places. That's the reason I took up my post across the street. I could see from where I was down to the corner. Anybody going in the back would have to pass around that way."

"You didn't think it was worthwhile to take up your post in the hall outside of Miss Hirzner's apartment, I suppose?" Tonelli asked.

"That was contrary to my orders, Lieutenant. The Captain down at the precinct told me I was not to be obnoxious and not to let none of the tenants know I was there and what I was doing."

Tonelli sighed. "I suppose you did the best you could. What time did you go to lunch?"

The man tried to give the appearance of thinking.

"I guess it was along about twelve o'clock. Maybe a few minutes before. But I didn't leave the place unguarded even then, Lieutenant. I got hold of the cop on the beat and told him to keep an eye on the place while I ran down and got a cup of coffee."

"How long did it take you to drink this cup of coffee?"

Once again the man strove to think deeply. "Well, I guess I was back a little before one o'clock, maybe it was a couple minutes after. You see, Lieutenant, my wife's gonna have a baby, and I called up to see how she was. That maybe took a little longer than I thought."

Tonelli swore. "Yeah, and while you were jabbering over the telephone to your wife, some slug walked in here and knocked this dame off. I don't care nothing about *your* job, but I certainly don't like to have my own shield pulled and go back to pounding the beat just because your wife's going to have a baby. I didn't have anything to do with it."

The man got dull brick-red.

"Well, go on," said Tonelli.

"That's all there is to it," the man said. "Nobody suspicious came in or out of the place while I was here, none of the house staff saw anybody, and the harness bull on the street didn't see anybody that didn't belong in the neighborhood."

"That lunkhead on the beat," Tonelli growled, "hasn't got any sense anyway. Who does he think *he* is, putting a ticket on my car for overtime parking?"

The Lieutenant got to his feet and began to prowl around the living room. Against one wall stood a secretary, and, facing it on the opposite side of the room, a mahogany commode, a modern reproduction of a colonial highboy. Tonelli opened the drawers of the commode one by one, rifling through their contents, mostly feminine clothes and household linens. He opened the secretary, went through the pigeonholes and drawers of the desk portion, glancing through the papers he found, then opened the upper section which had four shelves, the three upper ones filled with books. Tonelli stared intently at the bottom shelf, then turned on the luckless plain-clothesman again.

"You been snoopin' around here?" he demanded. "Have you taken anything off this shelf?"

"No, sir," the dick denied.

Tonelli beckoned to me, and pointed to the lower shelf. "Look at that."

Faint edges of dust showed that an oblong object roughly five inches by seven, had been lying on that particular shelf.

"What d'you suppose that was?" Tonelli asked.

"Might have been a paper or a card, a book, or a pamphlet," I guessed.

Tonelli took his handkerchief and wound it around the tip of his index finger. He whisked his covered finger across the center of the space left vacant, and held it up so I could see there was no dust.

"This apartment is as clean as a pin," said Tonelli. "There's very little dust on these books." He took one down and blew along its deckled edge to show me. "That means the inside of this bookcase is dusted every week or so. The dust is just about as thick on the edges of the shelves the books are on, as it is in the space from which this card or paper or whatever was removed. There's no dust in the square space itself. That means the object was removed within the last few hours. Otherwise there would have been a little bit of dust, enough to show."

I said, "Fine work, Sherlock. So what?"

"So," Tonelli said deliberately, "I'd be willing to bet you a couple of good drinks the guy that cracked this dame on the head is the guy that has in his possession the thing that was in this bookcase."

He went on prowl again, with me following him. In the bedroom he searched through the wardrobe and the chiffonier. In the bottom drawer of the chiffonier he found a pair of men's pajamas, a light dressing gown, and a pair of straw bedroom slippers. Both the pajamas and the dressing gown had initials embroidered on them, and the initials were "H.H.I."

"It's too bad," I said to Tonelli, "that Commodore Ireton didn't know more about the regulations of the WPA."

"What's the regulations of WPA got to do with this?" Pete asked.

"In Washington," I told him, "the first rule is that bosses do not sleep with the help."

"It's a good rule for any organization," said Tonelli.

Having made the full circuit of the apartment, not forgetting the bathroom where he pointed out a toothbrush kept separate from the ones in the rack above the washbasin, a man's safety razor and shaving cream, and other such intimate details of occupancy, Tonelli got on the telephone and called headquarters. Up to now he had made only emergency reports. This time he got the Chief, and made a complete report which he finished by requesting that the technical crew which had made a complete examination of the apartment while we were at the hospital, should give him all the data as soon as possible. He then admonished the whipped plainclothesman to see that nothing was disturbed, and especially to watch out for the news photographers when they came and keep them from lifting souvenirs of the love nest. All that disposed of:

"I'm running downtown to the laboratory," he said to me. "Do you want to go along and get the checkup on this incense pot?"

I'd forgotten the murder weapon which he had wrapped so carefully and placed in his pocket, but I was glad to go along with him.

He came stamping out of the laboratory after a considerable interval, chewing savagely on his cigar.

"What?" I asked.

"Nothing," he growled. "Only prints are old and faint. Evidently those of Sarah Hirzner herself, or maybe the maid. There's blood on it, human blood, and we'll check it up with Sarah Hirzner's just to be sure, but I know it's hers; and the hair is the same color and texture as hers."

"In other words," I jibed, "you know that Sarah Hirzner is dead, and she was killed with this incense burner which was alongside her bed."

"You said it," he admitted. "Come on, let's go over to the beerstube and get something to eat and a mug of beer."

It was half past six so I thought I might as well. There was nothing I could do at the office at that hour.

We drank a lot of beer, and talked and talked in circles. Tonelli went over and over the case, reviewing the facts, fitting things into place. He had accepted his own reconstruction of the crime, the first crime that is—the killing of the Administrator—and worked from there on.

"What I figure," he said, "is that this Hirzner dame *knew* too much. She was with the Commodore all day, and most of the nights. The guy that bumped the Commodore knew that, and he must also have known there was some kind of incriminating evidence in her apartment. Of course, we didn't make a minute search, but the expert squad hasn't turned up anything that we didn't see. My guess is there was a paper in that bookcase, something the murderer had to have. After he had killed the Commodore, he went around to see Sarah Hirzner. It was most likely incriminating evidence."

"Sounds reasonable," I murmured into my eighth stein of beer.

"There's one coincidence," Tonelli continued, "the murderer must have known Miss Hirzner almost as well, if not as well, as he did the Commodore. In both cases the victim allowed him to get up near enough to kill without being suspicious. That means he must have been somebody they saw all the time."

"You're describing about five hundred people," I said. "There are dozens of people in the WPA office who did business every day with the Administrator and his secretary. It might have been a messenger, or a guard, or one of the executives. It might have been a file clerk, or a stenographer."

"You're telling me," said Tonelli. He was very down. Beer made him melancholy. "There could have been a lot of people, like you say, on intimate terms with Ireton and the girl. But there can't be many people who would have been so vitally interested in a paper." He thought for a long while. "No," he said, "I don't believe Sarah saw the man who killed her. She was doped. The doctor gave her a sedative to make her sleep and rest. But, whoever killed her knew her well enough to know his way around in her apartment. He didn't rip anything apart in his search."

"Whatever was stolen wasn't very securely hidden," I said. "It was almost in plain sight."

"Sure," Tonelli agreed, "that means it wasn't valuable, or at least Sarah didn't know its value. It may have no value in itself, except as a clue."

"Did you measure the space in the bookcase that the stolen paper occupied?" I asked.

"No," said Tonelli. "It was about five by seven, though."

"That," I told him, "is the standard size for the large filing cards used in WPA. It might have been a record card, somebody's efficiency and service record. Hell, it might have been a whole stack of cards. It might have been a data card with some valuable inside dope on it."

"Sure," said Tonelli. "It might have been any of those things. And that helps a lot, don't it." He stared into his beer. "What were all those reports on the Commodore's desk?" he asked.

"Progress reports, from each of the projects. Some of them monthly, some semi-monthly, some weekly. Most of the Administrators have them boiled down by an assistant, but I'm told Ireton was a nut on that subject. He insisted upon reading every report himself, or at least skimming through it. It took him a lot of time. It took so much time he didn't have a chance to do much else. He estimated the value of a project and the amount of work it was doing by the size of the reports."

Tonelli grunted, "We've got some guys like that at headquarters."

I looked at the clock, and it was half past eleven. We had another beer, and Tonelli drove me to the hotel.

A batch of telephone calls, telegrams from Washington, and messages stuffed my letter box. Most of them were for me to call somebody, a dozen different somebodies, at the Administration Building. Because one or two of the wires had to be answered right away, I went around the corner to the Western Union office. By the time I finished there it was after twelve o'clock, and I was beginning to feel the day's excitement, the ten or twelve beers I'd consumed, and lost sleep. I went back to the hotel and started for my room.

The hotel was built in the shape of an E, with the foyer and elevator shafts occupying the central prong of the letter. My room was at the extreme end of the right-hand wing, and overlooked the street. There were about eight or ten rooms on either side of the corridor before you came to my door, which was the last one, in the corner. I noticed that one of the corridor ceiling lights was out, so that the corridor was lit only by the red exit light above the fire door. I paid no attention to it, and clasping my key and its tag together in my hand, moved merrily toward my own room. In the gloom I had to lean over to see the keyhole, and as I bent forward, something heavy swished past my head. The blow must have been started at the instant I bent over, for instead of clipping me on the bean it bounced off my shoulder.

No mean clout, even so. I went down with a thud, half stunned. I struggled back to my feet, shouting, but there was nobody in the hall by then. That hotel has good thick doors, soundproof walls, and uninquisitive tenants, for my shout failed to raise anybody. I glanced down at my feet, and stooped to pick up the club that had been used. It was the heavy brass nozzle of the fire hose from the rack on the wall. A nice weapon. If it had connected, I would have been exchanging confidences with Commodore Ireton and his inamorata in the Great Beyond. I opened the door and got into my room.

But I didn't stick my head in first. I reached cautiously around the doorjamb and snapped on the light. The room was empty, of course.

My shoulder felt like somebody had dropped a ton of bricks on it. I fingered it cautiously and discovered that nothing was broken. When I got my shirt off I could see that it would be beautifully black and blue by morning, and my left arm wouldn't be much good for a day or two.

After a hot bath and a swig of rum I crawled into bed, but the damn shoulder ached so badly I couldn't sleep. There was no reason in the world why I should suffer alone, so I called Ben Cook in Washington. For a wonder, he was at home.

"Well," I greeted him, "we've got another murder for you."

"Who is it this time?" he asked.

"Commodore Ireton's secretary and extracurricular-activity girl, Miss Sarah Hirzner."

"Who killed her?" asked Ben. "And why?"

"I have just come to the conclusion it was a mysterious man who hangs around in hotel corridors," I told him.

"Why don't you arrest him if you know who it is?" Ben demanded.

"I just found out," I said. "He's bounced the brass nozzle of a hose off my shoulder. He didn't aim so good at me. If he'd connected, you'd have had to have a new Deputy Administrator. And how's for a raise?"

Ben's tone changed. "Oh, go to bed, you lug," he said, "and sleep it off. Don't call me every time you get tight. I thought for a minute you were serious."

"Oh, no," I said, "just my little joke; but watch the morning papers anyway."

"If you were really assaulted, have you notified the police?" Ben asked.

I said sweetly, "Certainly not. You told me not to take any action. You told me to sit tight. To do nothing without instructions from Washington. Is it your instruction that I call the police and report this attack?"

"Go to hell," he said. So I hung up on him, and called Tonelli.

He wasn't half as excited as I thought he ought to be.

7

A LOT OF BUSINESS HAD FLOWED over the WPA dam while I was sleuthing around with Tonelli and having fun in the corridor. When I appeared at the office with my arm in a sling, I found the boys and girls, hoping to get in right with the new boss, had fixed me up a private office in what had been the Conference Room. The Commodore's old office was still under guard. I sat down to my desk and went over the routine mail with the aid of a taffy-haired gal with buck teeth whose name was Hilda. Whatever the underlying causes of unemployment may be, there are few good-looking stenogs on WPA payroll. The good lookers do all right in Private Industry regardless of skill. All the while I dictated I was going over the list of people in the office, trying to sift out one I could trust. I finally decided to trust nobody. I didn't know who was reporting to whom about what.

My letters finished, I wandered into the Assistant Administrator's office and found him talking to Captain Treadfast. I asked the pair of them to call a general staff meeting, as quickly as they could get the people together. I wanted all the chiefs of divisions, and the principal supervisors. They knocked me into a loop by reminding me the Commodore was to be buried at 10 o'clock, and that all the supervisors wanted would be at the funeral. Of course I had to go too. I gave instructions that as soon as the funeral services were over, I would expect all the supervisors to attend the conference. I made some joke to the effect that we could all hang together. It got no laughs. Everybody was sour because they had expected to chisel a half-day's leave on account of the burial.

Jaze Ireton glared when she saw me in the church, and a vinegar puss I set down as Aunt Margaret, who was with her, helped her to glare. Tonelli was there watching. I got away as quickly as was decent, and one by one my executive staff ambled into the conference. I gave them the old rah-rah pep talk about all working together for the good of the job and the glory of the old Stars and Stripes. It didn't make them swoon in ecstasy in the aisles, and inasmuch as they didn't appreciate my oratory I went to work sweating information out of them.

The result of that meeting was that by lunch time I had all of the important papers I could locate locked up, and special reports coming in showing the exact status of every job, from all directions.

Just before lunch Izzie stuck his head in my door. I was glad to see him. I motioned for him to come in, and he did, beaming.

"Congratulations," he said. "You can count on me to the last drop of my blood for cooperation and loyalty."

I said, "Sure. What's the new dirt?"

"There are two things," he said in his most confidential manner. "I have discovered that Mr. Lawrence Parsons is in love with Miss Ireton, the Commodore's daughter."

"Yes, he told me about it," I said.

Izzie's face fell.

"And you know, I suppose, that Miss Sarah Hirzner was very intimate with the Commodore?"

I tapped the morning paper on my desk, which headlined Sarah's murder. "That's not much of a secret any longer," I said. "You'll have to do better than that, Izzie."

Izzie approached confidentially, and remembering the little scene Tonelli and I had staged in the Commodore's office reconstructing the crime, I wheeled around in my chair so that I was facing him and he couldn't lean over me from the side and behind.

"I have very important information," said Izzie. "I have caught Mr. Bennington Graeme's assailant. Would you like to talk to him?"

I said, "Well, I guess that's a good idea. Where is he?"

"I will have to take you to him," Izzie said. "Shall I tell them to have your car brought around?"

"My car?" I questioned.

"O yes," said Izzie. "The Administrator's car is at your disposal."

I said, "That's ducky," and heaved myself out of the chair.

Izzie pretended to notice my arm in a sling for the first time. "Why, Mr. Moore!" he exclaimed. "Did you injure your arm?"

"Yes," I said, "while I was shaving this morning the razor flew into a rage and bit me."

Izzie looked incredulous.

My official car, I found, was a Packard limousine of the vintage of 1934, with plum-colored cushions. Izzie and I piled in, and Izzie gave sailing directions to a street down in the river district. It took twenty-five minutes of fast driving to get there.

We stopped at last in front of a warehouse building, one of those old red-brick structures built in the early '90s. Izzie led the way through a side door, up a long flight of stairs, to an office on the second floor. It was no surprise to me to find my old friend Charlie the Poet sitting in a chair with two WPA guards glowering at him.

Izzie waved toward this ensemble with the self-satisfied smirk of an impresario. It was an effective grouping. Izzie knew his dramatic values. I made a mental note to suggest him to Mrs. Flood.

"So this is the fellow that slugged Mr. Graeme," I said.

The answer came not from Izzie, Charlie, or the two guards, but from the doorway behind me. Lieutenant Tonelli said:

"Yes, that's the guy." He came in and nodded to Izzie. "Thank you very much," he said sarcastically. "The Police Department is mighty busy these days. Pretty white of you to go out and pick up this lug for us."

"Evidently," I said, "you've got some dicks on the force that don't have to go out and get a cup of coffee every now and then."

Tonelli grunted.

"I'd be very much obliged to you," I said, "if you'd have a city ordinance passed compelling all hotels to use soft rubber nozzles on fire hoses, and if you would detail a special squad to see that the ordinance is carried out."

"What's the matter, does your arm hurt?" Tonelli asked.

I thumbed my nose at him with my good hand.

Tonelli reached out, caught hold of the back of the chair in which one of the guards sprawled, and dumped him out of it. He took the chair and planted it with its back facing the prisoner, and then straddled the seat resting his arms across the back of the chair and his chin on his wrists. He stared unwinkingly at Charlie for a long moment or two. Silently two plainclothesmen drifted into the room, gestured to the guards and Izzie to get out, and took their stations— one on each side, and a little to the rear of their Lieutenant. Tonelli thumbed Izzie and the two WPA guards out of the room before he spoke to the prisoner.

"How much did you get for this job?" he asked.

Charlie muttered stupidly, "What job?"

"Weren't you in on the job to beat up Mr. Graeme?" Tonelli demanded.

"Never heard of any such job," said Charlie.

Tonelli stared at him for another lengthy space.

"How many men were there in on it with you?"

"In on what?" Charlie asked.

One of the men behind Tonelli reached over suddenly and slapped Charlie in the face. "Cut it out, lug," he said, "You socked the man, didn't you?"

Charlie pulled back sullenly. "What man?" he asked.

Between my teeth I said, "So you won't talk, eh?"

I walked out of the room and joined Izzie in my limousine below. We waited there for three quarters of an hour. At the end of that time Charlie came staggering out, prodded by the two plainclothesmen, with Tonelli bringing up the rear. The Lieutenant came over to the car, leaned on the window sill, and lit a fresh cigar.

"Wrong number," he said. "This mug didn't slug Graeme, but he knows who did. Follow me down to Headquarters. He's going to give a statement, and I thought you might like to hear it."

Suddenly Izzie began to fidget. "If you don't mind," he said, "I think I better get back to the office."

"That's all right by me," I gave him my blessing. Izzie popped out of the car and down the street so fast you could play marbles on his flying coattails.

Tonelli remarked, "That baby wants to get some place in a hurry."

"You tell me all about it tomorrow, when you get your daily report on him," I suggested.

The procedure at headquarters was rather tame. Charlie was completely and thoroughly subdued. He answered all questions like a little man, without stalling, and when he was asked to dictate a statement he started right in as if he'd been used to stenographers all his life. The statement went something like this:

"I didn't have nothing to do with slugging and drowning Mr. Bennington Graeme. I was at a party where Mr. Graeme was, and I seen him leave. The next day I seen in the papers where he had been slugged. That is all I know about the slugging.

"Some guys I know down on the docks sometimes gets little extra jobs to do. One of these guys whose name I don't know except that everybody calls him 'Butch,' was talking to me in Mac's place and he told me he and another mug had a job to do. He said he was told to go to a certain street where he would find a car and a driver. He and his friend went to this street, and found a car and a driver. The driver had two envelopes and each of the envelopes had twenty-five bucks in them. The driver told them they were going to go to another place and wait till a guy came out of a house. The driver said he would finger this guy and one of them in the car should call out to this guy and offer him a ride. When he got in the car he was to be slugged, and the driver would tell them what else to do. They done this and then they drove the guy to a dock and dumped him overboard. They was told not to kill the guy, only sock him good and duck him for a scare."

Tonelli was satisfied with this statement. He said to Charlie, "Didn't your pal have any description of this guy he was to slug?"

Charlie said, "Yes. He said they told him the guy was about five feet ten inches tall, and he was wearing a dark gray overcoat and a gray hat. He had black hair."

Tonelli looked at me. "That's a good description of Mr. Graeme," he said, "and it fits you too."

I lit a cigarette.

They let Charlie go, and I left too. I drove immediately back to the Administration Building. The car didn't drive as fast going home as it had going downtown. As we turned into a side street south of the Administration Building, a man ran out of a small cigar store near the corner. He pulled up short on the curb and let fly. I ducked, and yelled to the driver to put on speed. A nice big chunk of cobble-stone came thudding onto the floor of the car, and the window at my side was beyond repair. The driver didn't seem to think this was so terrible. He took it calmly. We pulled up at the curb in front of the Building, and he asked:

"Will you need me any more tonight, Mr. Moore?"

"No," I said. "You better drive around and have a new window put in."

Upstairs in my office I found three or four people waiting, but I shooed them away and told the bucktoothed stenographer to get me Izzie. In a few minutes the door opened slowly, and Izzie edged into the room. I was standing by the desk. I walked over to him with my right hand outstretched. As Izzie reached for it, I slipped my left out of the sling to lead with, and smacked him flush on the chin with my right. He went down in a heap. I flexed my shoulder and got my hand back in the sling. I shouldn't have used that arm.

Izzie sat up on the floor and slowly rubbed his chin.

"What was that for?" he asked.

"That was because I'm five feet ten inches tall," I said sweetly, "and because I wear a dark gray coat and a gray hat and have black hair and went to the same party with Bennington Graeme. You remember—you took me to the party. It's also because I don't like official cars that get cobblestones flung in 'em, and I do not care for hose nozzles. From now on I ride taxis, and I choose my own cabs."

Izzie boosted himself to his feet.

"Will you want anything more tonight?" he asked.

I said, "Good night."

He closed the door softly behind him. But in a moment he poked his head back in. "If you wanna know," he said, "I was the guy that threw Mr. Bennington Graeme the rope end when he was drowning. I pulled him out of the river, and saved him from drowning."

"Okay," I said, "I'll see that you're recommended for the Carne-gie Medal."

He left for good on that.

WHEN I GOT BACK TO MY HOTEL that night the clerk told me there was a man waiting to see me. It was Matthew Van Gelder, one of the directors who had sat in on my first, last, and only conference with

Commodore Ireton. Mr. Van Gelder was a small, neat gentleman who ran to spats and a pince-nez with black ribbon. He also wore a black Homburg hat and Oxford gray jacket with striped trousers. He was so neat and dressy, fussed so needlessly with his eyeglasses, I put him down for a nance. He seemed to be in his forties, but his hair, which was rather sparse, was still yellow and did not match his sallow complexion and brown eyes.

"Good evening, Mr. Van Gelder," I said. "What can I do for you?"

He swung his glasses hesitantly and came to the point, speaking with that breathless rush that so many diffident people acquire.

"It seemed to me that it was only right for me to—er—report, or rather, to present to you some facts for your information. As the new Administrator—"

"Only Acting Deputy Administrator," I put in.

"However that may be, at least you are the official representative of the Federal Government here," he said.

I nodded.

"I would like to place myself on record, and to inform you exactly how matters stood between me and the late Commodore Ireton," he said officiously.

I murmured something about being very happy to hear anything he had to say. I suggested I was hungry, and invited him to come and have dinner with me.

"Oh no, no," he said. "I make it a point to eat rather early, but I'll be glad to have a cup of coffee with you while *you* are having dinner."

When the business of ordering was over, I said, "Now, Mr. Van Gelder."

"Perhaps," he said, "it would give you a better idea exactly how I stood with the late Administrator to tell you as nearly in detail as I may the circumstances of our last interview alone, a few days before his death."

I sat back in my chair prepared to suffer.

"There is probably a great deal to be said in defense of Commodore Ireton," said Mr. Van Gelder charitably. "I understand he was kind, considerate, and even generous to those who were near him. His daughter, and his secretary, Miss Sarah Hirzner, for instance." He added parenthetically: "Shocking business, her death, wasn't it?"

"Yes," I admitted.

"His close friends, I believe, say his wife simply worshipped him and that it was only after her death the Commodore became the irascible, neurotic person you and I knew."

"I didn't know the Commodore; I met him for the first time when I came from Washington three days ago," I informed him, to keep the record straight.

"I must say, however," said Mr. Van Gelder firmly, "that in his relationships with his colleagues in the WPA he was almost impossible. In fact, I might go so far as to say he was quite impossible."

I muttered, "We have come to bury Caesar, not to praise him."

Mr. Van Gelder spoke up, "I beg your pardon?"

"Pay no attention," I told him. "It's a habit of mine, talking to myself. Go right ahead, Mr. Van Gelder. I'm very much interested to hear what happened at the interview you had with him."

"To come directly to the point," Mr. Van Gelder said, and I hoped that he meant it, "I argued with him for, I should say, upward of forty minutes in my last interview with him. You see he had an idea that the problem of all unemployed workers was the same; he had a fixed impression that the men who were unemployed were in that sad condition because they were inimical to the interests of private employers and of the State. In short, he thought that the greatest number of WPA workers were Communists, or worse."

"What *could* be worse?" I asked wide-eyed. He was impervious to sarcasm.

"If you are not familiar with the gradations of radicalism," Mr. Van Gelder offered to enlighten me, "I may say that there are men who are far more extreme in their views than the followers of Marx, Lenin and Stalin."

"I should be glad to hear about it," I said. The soup had arrived, and I didn't feel I was wasting my time. He might as well babble on.

"Because of this unhappy fixation of the Commodore's, he evolved the most far-reaching and pernicious system of spies and secret police in the projects. Now, Mr. Moore, you are a reasonable man—"

I choked on a spoonful of soup.

"—therefore you will understand me when I say that there is a great deal of uneasiness, a great deal of loose talking, a great deal of unrest, in our WPA projects. This is particularly true of the white-collar projects. In my own division I have men and women who have been out of work for two and three years. Competent people, with university degrees, and capable minds. These people's point of view is warped—"

The fish course had arrived, and as I dabbled in the shrimp sauce I ventured to suggest that I had read reports on the projects, and that I would like to come to the immediate matter of Mr. Van Gelder's last interview with Commodore Ireton.

"Yes, yes, of course," he smiled. "One becomes so enthused in this work, so much interested in the welfare of one's people, that one forgets that this is a twice-told tale to those of you who have seen it in its larger aspect."

The man talked like a preacher.

"You could imagine how I felt, then, when I suggested that it would be a good idea to put additional people on my project in re-search work, and found that in spite of the fact that there are many needy in this class in the city, the Commodore rejected the idea with scorn. He actually snorted. 'White-collar people. It's time they got their collars dirty! By God, they ought to be glad to dig ditches in order to eat!' Really, Mr. Moore, you have no idea how that man cursed and swore. Every other word he said was profanity. With all due allowances to his great physical pain, and the bitterness in his life, I'm certain there was no provocation for such language as he used. It is really no wonder he was killed. Indeed you know Sarah Hirzner, his secretary, often said his cursing tongue would succeed in getting him killed."

"There was a prophet who should have been honored in her own country," I remarked.

"I have repeated this little scene to you simply to give you an idea of how difficult it was to get along with the Commodore, and if you can understand something of his attitude it will be easier for you to believe what I am going to tell you."

"Oh," I said, "is there more?" I dug into my roast beef au jus.

"In my own project I first became aware of the state of affairs; and when I inquired among my friends and the directors, I found that they too were troubled with the same sort of thing. The first

evidence was a weekly newspaper, got out by a group of the workers on my project, in mimeographed form. It was called 'The Four-
Square American.' The first issue seemed a rather harmless, platitu-
dinous affair. It urged the workers to join a national organization of
Four-Square Americans, and to exhibit their insignia, which was a
purple square worn in the buttonhole. The objectives of this national
organization were to reduce unemployment nationally, and to back
up the provisions of the Constitution of the United States."

"That hasn't yet become a hanging matter," I remarked. "It's not
even against the law to recite the Declaration of Independence."

"Oh no, indeed," Mr. Van Gelder hastened to agree, "the objectives of this organization at first, and indeed all the time, were quite
laudable. But the methods suggested of achieving it began to take on
more than a tinge of foreign influence. Before the organization was
two weeks old, a uniformed corps of Four-Square Americans was in
the progress of formation, the uniform consisting of black felt hats,
purple shirts, and blue denim overall pants."

"All children like to play soldiers, Mr. Van Gelder," I soothed
him.

"This was far from play, I can assure you, Mr. Moore," he said
tartly. "To my dismay I soon found that out. I was working late in the
office one evening when some ten or fifteen of these men, dressed
in uniform, entered. They were all masked. They placed a list on my
desk of the names of several men on my project who, they demanded,
must be dismissed forthwith."

"They knew what they wanted, didn't they?" I said.

"Indeed they did," said Mr. Van Gelder. "They then made further
demands that all persons hired by the WPA on my project should
first pass the scrutiny of a committee of Four-Square Americans.
The death of Commodore Ireton and your accession to the Administrator's position leaves them doubtful—and indeed, leaves us directors doubtful—as to the wise and safe course to pursue."

"And so you, I assume, have dropped in this evening to find out
exactly what my attitude is toward this sort of thing?" I said.

Mr. Van Gelder raised both hands in protest. "Please, please," he
said. "Do not think I am in sympathy with these men."

"So far as I know," I told him, "nothing in the common law or the regulations of the Works Progress Administration forbids men to join unions, fraternal organizations, or any other peaceful, law-abiding group, as long as they do not do it on Government time."

"Ah, but they do!" said Mr. Van Gelder. "And not only that, but they were encouraged to organize and to hold meetings, keep their books, and carry on their business during Project working hours."

"Who encouraged them?" I asked.

Mr. Van Gelder sank his voice two octaves. "Commodore Ireton," he breathed.

"We heard something of this kind of thing in Washington," I said, "but we didn't believe it or dream that it went to these lengths."

"I can assure you it is all I say, and more," said Mr. Van Gelder. "Not only that, but through his system of spies Commodore Ireton was rapidly stamping out free speech and initiative on the projects. Every known sympathizer to liberal tenets and creeds was marked down by Commodore Ireton's men, and 'taken care of' either by them or by the Four-Square Americans. There has been a great deal of *this* sort of thing going on."

Mr. Van Gelder triumphantly laid his egg in front of me. It was an ordinary five by seven Governmental record card, headed "JAMES MOULTRIE MOORE," and remarks under that heading read:

"James Moultrie Moore; born Mooretown, Georgia, August 31, 1900. Educated Mooretown schools and Southern Record College. Post-graduate, Columbia University, M.A. degree in Economics. Instructor in Economics, Nanking University, China, 1925-1927. Assistant Professor of Economics, Coketown Polytechnic Institute, 1927-1929. Was member of Arbitration Board and Survey, bituminous coal miners' strike 1929. Requested to resign from Coketown faculty 1929, due to political activity in behalf of iron and steel workers' unions. Feature writer for World Affairs Press Syndicate, 1930-1933. Labor and economics expert for *Evening Blade*, 1933-1935. Appointed through Benjamin Cook as special expert and advisor on economics and labor for WPA, June 1935."

"This seems a fair statement of the facts," I said after I had read it.

"It was not intended as such," Mr. Van Gelder assured me. "This card came from what is known as the Suspect File. That was a file

kept in Commodore Ireton's office, locked, and with keys in possession only of the Commodore and of his secretary, Miss Sarah
Hirzner. The names of the people and records in this file were intended to be used as evidence against those listed."

"Evidence for what?" I demanded.

"I am reliably informed," said Mr. Van Gelder, speaking like a
Washington correspondent, "that when the Four-Square Americans
found themselves strong enough they intended to hold what they
call a 'kangaroo court.' And to see that those convicted by this court
of un-Americanism were ridden out of town on a rail, and possibly
tarred and feathered."

"Cheery boys," I remarked. "They're handy with cobblestones,
too."

"That I know nothing of," Mr. Van Gelder assured me. "My
knowledge of them is purely hearsay."

"You got an earful," I congratulated him. "Tell me, how did you
come to be in possession of this card?"

"To the best of my belief," Mr. Van Gelder now talked like an expert on the witness stand, "this card was removed from the file when
word was received that you were coming here from Washington. It
was passed on to a committee of the Four-Square Americans. A man
in my project whom I believe to be very active in the organization,
was taken ill during working hours. We have no proper first-aid
facilities, and what medicines we have are kept in my office. He
was carried into my office, where we made him as comfortable as
we might, and while I was doing for him what I could, pending the
arrival of the doctor, this card dropped out of his inside pocket."

"I would like to have a long and serious conversation with this
man," I said.

Van Gelder nodded wisely. "You'll have to wait," he said. "The
man is out on sick leave at the moment, but at your convenience and
upon his return I'll be glad to arrange an interview with him in your
office or in mine."

"That's very kind of you, Mr. Van Gelder," I spoke around my last
mouthful of ice cream. "May I keep this card?"

"Oh, certainly," said Mr. Van Gelder graciously. "By all means."

"Have you any more information?" I asked as I slid my tip under the plate. "Anything more that you can add?"

He rose with me. "Nothing essential at the moment. However, I shall keep you informed. I thought that this was a matter that should be brought to your personal attention as quickly as possible. I have tried to contact you at your office, but I have been persistently informed that you were out. That's the reason why I took the liberty of coming here to your hotel."

"How did you find out this was my hotel?" I asked as I walked him through the lobby toward the front door.

"Oh, that was very easy," he informed me. "I called up Izzie Jones. I suppose you know Izzie?"

"Very well indeed," I said. "He seems to be a valuable and most versatile person."

We told each other good-night politely, after I had thanked him for his solicitude and information.

The light was burning brightly in the corridor outside my room, but the hotel had not yet discovered the brass nozzle on the fire hose was missing.

8

THE NUMBER OF TIMES beautiful ladies have waked me up in the middle of the night I can count on my thumbs, and do. This was one of them. In a pleased, if scandalized, voice the night clerk informed me Miss Ireton was calling. When I suggested he send her up, he reminded me this was a respectable hotel. So I had to get almost dressed and go downstairs.

Jaze was in a fine dither. It had just begun to dawn upon her that she had been largely instrumental in putting her boy friend into a position where he might easily spend the rest of his life on the inside looking out. That I was prepared for; but I was hardly prepared to find she hadn't seen Larry Parsons since the riot in the Administration Building.

"Why did you deny you knew him?" I asked her, "when Tonelli's men questioned you about him?"

She wept. "I was all unstrung. We had been keeping it a secret so long that I suppose my lies about it were automatic."

"I suggest you let me go back to sleep, and you go to Lieutenant Tonelli in the morning and tell your troubles to him," I said.

She hesitated. "But he'll ask me so many questions."

"Nobody," I informed her sententiously, "need be afraid of the truth if they're innocent. Did you murder your father?"

That unleashed the hounds of hell.

She sprang up, her cheeks aflame, her fingers like a tiger's talons. She was exactly as she had been outside the Administration Building when she had found me by the litter in which they were carrying her father's dead body.

"You! You fiend in human form"—I thought this was a little movie-ish, but somehow it didn't seem too much out of place in a dingy hotel parlor at three-thirty in the morning—"I think you put him up to it. I think it's an official plot. All of you Reds and Communist sympathizers hated my father."

"Whom did we put up to what?" I was actually bewildered.

"Larry," she flashed out. "He's not really like this. He's a nice man at heart. He doesn't want to be a Communist. He thinks it's smart and advanced to be a Communist. He—all you clever people have imposed on him. You've made him think your way. You shoved him forward as a puppet. I know what happens. My father's told me many times what happens."

"What?" I asked, honestly interested.

"Your technique. Whenever any of you people in Washington want anything from the President or from Congress, do you go and ask for it like men? Not a bit of it. You and your undercover people up here. They talk to this one, and to that one. They go to secret meetings and make speeches. And then the first thing you know the workers are making demonstrations. Holding sit-down strikes. Forming picket lines. Then you go rushing to the President and Congress and say that the *workers* demand increases in appropriations and all the while you put them up to it."

"It's a good idea," I congratulated her. "I'll certainly pass it along. I'm afraid, however, you credit Washington with being too Machiavellian. They're really simple and fairly honest people."

If a lady might be said to snort, she did. She would have none of it. She railed and raved. From top to bottom, in her opinion, the Administration, particularly of the relief program, was riddled with radical ideas and leaders.

"Why is it," she asked me, "whenever Larry goes to Washington he is invariably advised to come back here and *fight* for what he wants?"

"Probably because that's the only way he'll get it," I tried to explain. "You see, there's more to this than meets the naked eye. After all, Congress holds the purse strings, and your Congressman hears nothing but the voice of the people. That's why he keeps his ear to the ground. He doesn't want to hear too much. The voice of the people has to get so loud as to be practically deafening before he will lift his ear from the ground long enough to listen."

"That's what I hate about you," she said intensely, "your flippancy. And cynicism. All of you have it. Lawrence is getting that way too. And I can't stand it! And now, you've egged him on to kill my father."

"Hush! Not so loud," I begged her. "Somebody might hear you and believe you."

From her high horse she descended into a lachrymose depth. She begged me to tell her it wasn't so. That Larry hadn't killed her father. Yet when I assured her he hadn't, she only wept the more.

"Very well," I said at last. I was tired and sleepy. "I'll confess. *I* killed him. Now go home and go to bed. Get some rest, and in the morning we'll go down to headquarters and tell all. Then you can get the Bureau of Missing Persons to look for Larry, and you both can be happy ever after while I hang."

That quieted her. She got up from the sofa and backed away from me to the door, clutching her handbag with both hands. At the door, ready to run, she said breathlessly:

"Where will you be tomorrow morning to confess?"

"If you'll promise to take two aspirins and a teaspoonful of soda in water as soon as you get home," I bargained, "I'll guarantee to be at headquarters by nine-thirty a.m."

"I promise," she said in a very small voice, ducked, and was gone.

Humor never pays with women.

MURDERER CONFESSES TO VICTIM'S DAUGHTER. So the far flung eight-column banner across the first page of the *Morning News*, in an extra edition. That little fool went right from the hotel to the *News* office, and spilled everything I'd told her. They wanted to believe her, and they had this silly extra on the street by six-thirty in the morning. I got no sleep at all after that. Every newshound in the city was clamoring to talk to me. Tonelli got to the hotel at seven o'clock, and literally he had to fight his way into my room. Then, for my own good, he arrested me and took me down to the District Attorney's office. He sent out for breakfast for me, and I ate it while

I was waiting for the D.A. to show up. Between Tonelli and me we convinced the D.A. the girl was a little balmy. Then we discussed what was best to do.

Being a lawyer, the D.A. had a strong conviction that everything else should wait while I entered suit against Jaze for defamation of character. Finally Tonelli solved the question by producing Larry Parsons. He sent out and got Jaze Ireton and confronted the two of them. It was a very wise move. Twenty minutes alone together brought out Jaze repentant and frightened. The reporter who covered headquarters for the *News* agreed, after consulting the managing editor, that they would retract all statements and apologize in headlines as big as they had printed the libel. Big generous me agreed not to sue Jaze nor the *News*. But my sleep was gone forever.

This thing was getting under my skin like a chigger. It didn't help any to find a sheaf of scathing telegrams from Ben Cook on my desk at the office. Action was indicated for me. I called in Izzie.

Carefully I locked the door, which didn't do much good because the flimsy partitions in my office afforded no privacy. In my state of mind, the more people who heard what I had to say, the better. The locked door was only to add glamour and mystery and make them listen harder.

"Sit in that chair," I ordered Izzie. He sat.

I got a nice long sharp paper knife from the desk, and stood over Izzie with it.

"Take a good look at this," I invited.

"Yes sir," he said.

"Do you think it would do the business for you if I were to stick it in your jugular?"

"Yes sir," he said.

"Very well, then. Start to talk."

Izzie started. He said practically nothing. He babbled.

"When I say talk," I enlightened him, "I do not mean that I am in love with your dulcet tones. I don't want music, I want information."

"Yes sir," he said.

"What is behind all this mystery and killing?" I demanded.

Izzie looked scared and said nothing.

I threw the paper knife back on the desk.

"This is a waste of time," I said. "I'm sorry if I've acted childish. I can't go through with it. I guess I'm not the stuff hardboiled cops are made of."

"Yes sir," said Izzie.

I got hold of Tonelli, who promised to come right over, and I kept Izzie sitting there until the Lieutenant arrived.

"Now, Lieutenant," I said, very official, "we're not going to play with this thing any more. I've been doing this and that, and telling you what I thought you ought to know, and trying to cover up your scandal, and all that's happened is I've made things worse. It's time to take the lid off. Let's find out what makes the business tick and stink. Start to work on Izzie. He's the key to the whole thing, I'll swear."

Tonelli sighed. "You're about two days too early," he demurred. "The thing's not ripe yet. I wish you'd give me two more days."

"In two more days I'd be in the booby-hatch," I snapped.

"By the way," Tonelli spoke with seeming irrelevance, "we were wrong about that dust mark in Sarah Hirzner's bookcase. The boys measured it. It was not 5 by 7, but 6¼ by 8."

"So what?" I asked.

"Thought maybe you might be interested," Tonelli said carelessly.

"Why?" I demanded.

Tonelli shook his head and moved over to Izzie. He stabbed Izzie in the midriff with a husky forefinger.

"You been saving any gents from drowning since you pulled Mr. Graeme out of the river?" he asked.

Izzie glowered.

"Bad mistake you made there," Tonelli said. "These mixed identities always end bad for everybody involved."

"I had nothing to do with it," Izzie denied.

Tonelli strolled around the office.

"You know, chief," he said to me, "I think it'd be a good idea if you'd call a staff meeting."

"What kind of a staff meeting?" I asked.

"Just a staff meeting," Tonelli waved his arms largely.

"Do you know," I asked him, "that there are six hundred supervisors and section chiefs in the WPA in this city?"

"You got a lease on the Bijou Theatre," said Tonelli easily. "That holds nine-hundred-and-some people."

With bad grace I took up the telephone and told the Assistant Administrator to have the entire supervisory personnel of the WPA in the district report to the Bijou Theatre the following morning at nine o'clock. No excuses would be accepted, I said, unless it was a certificate of disability signed by two reputable physicians. Any one not disabled who failed to show up would be dismissed forthwith. I got an argument, but it was arranged. Then I turned on Tonelli. He smiled irritatingly and hummed, "Oy, Marie."

"Any special arrangements, Lieutenant Tonelli?" I asked sarcastically.

Carefully de-cellophaning a bad cigar, he said, "No thanks. I've already made my arrangements."

"Very nice of you to let me in on the tail end of them," I said.

"You might as well go home and get some sleep," Tonelli grinned. "You haven't had much in the last few days."

That was very sound advice, and I took it.

TWENTY-SEVEN OF THE BOSSES failed to show up at our theatre party. Seven of them were in hospital, the other twenty, the welfare worker assured me, were so close to being sick it made little difference. When they were all assembled, I walked out on the apron of the stage and made a little speech.

"Ladies and gentlemen," I said, "all of you know that the Administrator has been murdered. That his secretary has been murdered. That the head of the Writers' Project was assaulted. Some of you know, perhaps, that attacks have been made upon me. Lieutenant Tonelli of the police has asked me to bring you all here together. I have no idea what he wants, but I shall now turn the meeting over to him."

Tonelli, standing in the orchestra pit, said, "Get up there, Hogan, and read that list."

A beefy cop climbed up on the stage and stood at one side with a long typewritten list in his hand. Tonelli turned to the audience and ordered:

"As Patrolman Hogan reads out these names, I want the man or the woman to stand up, and remain standing."

Hogan began reading. There were a lot of names. Fifty-two, I found out later. With a great deal of hesitancy among the first ones, man after man began standing up. They were all men. As Hogan got well into his list, there was a tendency for men to stand up before their names were called. I caught two men in the front rows exchanging signals of some sort. Hogan's bull voice boomed through the V's and W's, and stopped.

As if this were a signal, the standees broke into a concerted cheer.

"*Four-Square is fore-armed! Nail Old Glory to the top of the pole! Hurrah!*"

Tonelli waited until the shouting had died down.

"You have answered all my questions by that cheer," he told the audience. "Is there any other Four-Square American who would like to join this group?"

There was no stir from the rest of the audience.

"You men who are standing will walk quietly to the rear of the theatre," Tonelli ordered. "And then downstairs to the men's lounge in the basement. You'll stay there until further orders."

The men filed out. Some of them muttering and growling, and there were catcalls and jeers from the rest of the audience; but no real demonstration on either side.

At each head of an aisle stood a policeman. All the exits were guarded. It would have been futile to have resisted.

I dropped down into the orchestra pit alongside of Tonelli while the men were leaving.

"What's the big idea?" I asked.

"You'll see," he promised.

"If you only wanted those fifty or so, why did you have me take all these people from their work?"

Tonelli only repeated, "You'll see. I'll explain."

The trampling and the stamping, the catcalls, the jeers, and the noise died down. Patrolman Hogan shouted "Silence!" in a voice that shook the proscenium.

"Friends," Tonelli began to make a speech. "I've asked you here to cooperate with the police. I'll begin by promising you complete protection. We have reason to believe there is a gigantic racket in process in the WPA. We believe that many of you have been victimized, that you are paying protection to keep your jobs, under the impression that you have to do so. I call on Mr. Moore to assure you that this is not the case. If you are legally entitled to your positions, you are not beholden to any influence, political or otherwise, for keeping your job. Is that right, Mr. Moore?"

"That's right," I said.

"Is that official?" Tonelli insisted. "Will you assure these people out here that they will not get into any trouble if they give the police the information we need?"

"I can assure everyone here officially," I said, "that the WPA is back of the police one hundred percent, that every employee of the WPA who in any way can aid or advise the police is not only requested but will be required to do so."

"Now folks," Tonelli took up the burden, "I'll tell you some things, and if you know anything that will help us in our investigation, all you have to do is to write your name and address on a piece of paper and either hand it to me, or to any uniformed policeman in the house, or mail it to Headquarters addressed to me. We'll fix it so you can give your testimony in private, and not even your wife need know about it."

A few nervous titters at that, followed by dead silence, while Tonelli took a deep breath and prepared to go on.

"The police have been informed, and our preliminary investigations lead us to believe, there is a dangerous and illegal organization operating in the midst of WPA. Certain unscrupulous men have banded together in an organization which they have extended from top to bottom of your ranks. Under the pretense of being a patriotic order, they have begun to victimize and terrorize their fellow workers. If any of you know anything about any such organization, you should report what you know to the police. And do it immediately. Remember what I said. All you have to do is put your name on a piece of paper and hand it to a cop."

Tonelli stopped short. I waited, but apparently he had completed his address.

"You've heard what Lieutenant Tonelli had to say," I finally broke the silence. "Perhaps there is someone here now who would care to make a statement, or who has some comment."

After some stirrings, whisperings, mutterings, a slim solitary figure stood up.

I peered through the gloom of the house.

"Mr. Matthew Van Gelder," I recognized him. "You have something you would like to say?"

Mr. Van Gelder adjusted his pince-nez, threw back his head, and spoke in a bravura tone:

"I do not need the protection of the law to do my duty as a citizen. I do not have to write my name upon a silly scrap of paper. Whatever I have to say may be said in the open."

"Whatever you say, whatever you do that is within the law, you can be dead sure of protection from the police," Tonelli interposed reassuringly.

"I have already made a report—a semi-official report—I am sure Mr. Moore will bear me out," pontificated Mr. Van Gelder. "And I wish to go on record at this moment as being of the opinion that there is not only one but two dangerous organizations in WPA. There is Four-Square, and there is a Communist group. Everyone here is aware of their existence. I for one volunteer openly to place any information I may have gathered about either one at the disposal of the authorities, and I hope that everyone here present will follow my example."

"Thank you, Mr. Van Gelder," I said. "I'm sure Lieutenant Tonelli will be glad to hear what you have to tell him. Is there anybody else?"

Some confusion in the audience, with a lot of whispering and chattering, and then a voice at the back of the house boomed, "I know something." Another said, "So do I." In an instant there were a dozen people, and then perhaps fifty clamoring to be heard.

Hogan unleashed his diapason bass.

"Quiet!"

In the lull, Tonelli spoke again. "Leave your names with the officers, or with me," he said. "That is all."

It was a good three quarters of an hour before the last person had given his name. Then I turned to Tonelli.

"What about your friends?"

"What friends?" Tonelli asked innocently.

There was no use trying to get a rise out of Tonelli in that mood. I said, "The men downstairs."

"Go down and take a look," Tonelli invited. "There isn't anybody downstairs."

I said, "Oh no? What happened to them?"

"There is a stairway leading from the lounge to the lobby," Tonelli smirked. "While we were having our little party here, my boys unloaded those babies into the wagons. They are safely in the precinct jail. In fact, I've got a squad over there waiting for 'em. They oughta know something by now. You want to go over?"

I said, "Yeah, I'd like to go over."

"I didn't really have to stage that show," Tonelli confessed. "But I thought it would be kinda fun and might save some serious trouble. You see these Four-Squares have a big organization. I didn't know if I had all of the leaders on that list. So I pretended they was just going downstairs, and kept the rest of them upstairs answering questions. They may give us some evidence but I think I got all I need to convict right now."

9

THAT WAS A WEIRD GATHERING. Tonelli's men had sifted through the chaff, and by the time we arrived had selected three men whose stories they were checking one against the other. These stories were so much alike, they can be given as one.

I don't mind telling you, that was a yarn. This Four-Square organization was something to write home about. First off, there was the symbolism of the square. The top bar stood for Country; one of the side bars was Religion; the other one was Loyalty; and the bottom one stood for the Family. And All American.

On paper they had divided up the country into Four-Square military districts, corresponding to the divisional lines of the United States Army. They modestly announced to their membership they were a citizen army whose purpose was to prepare to leap to arms and fortify the regular army in time of great national peril. Their advantage over the regular reserve lay in the fact that they did not have to wait for foolish folderols of the President and Congress in order to mobilize. They could mobilize at the drop of a hat, and they weren't particular whose hat it was.

Their hierarchy was established from the top down. Above all and foremost stood a mysterious Leader, known as General Z. From him emanated all plans, and all authority. They had invited Colonel Lindbergh to be Field Marshal commanding the air forces, and every other flier who made the Sunday papers was offered a commission as a general. There is no record that any of them accepted.

Admiral Byrd was to be a full Admiral commanding the naval forces. He too had not accepted. Many other key dignitaries of past or potential naval and military fame were commissioned on paper as staff officers, chiefs of divisions, brigade commanders; none of them with a grade lower than General. The fifty-two Tonelli had netted in his theatre party were active officers. They were all Colonels or Majors of the land forces, or Commanders and Lieutenant-Commanders, where they had naval experience. They claimed a total voluntary enrollment in the local WPA alone of 4,000 and while they waited anxiously for a national cataclysm which would call for their full and strictly imaginary strength of 5,000,000 men they contented themselves with shaking down members and non-members of the local Works Progress Administration.

The uniform racket in itself netted them a pretty penny. They bought purple shirts and overalls wholesale, and retailed them to the membership at two or three hundred per cent mark-up. Kick-backs on salary were paid regularly by workers terrorized by threats of losing their jobs or of physical violence. All of this money was turned in to Unit Commanders, who deducted a percentage and passed the take to the next higher up who, in turn, paid it over to a Treasurer; and this worthy delivered in cash to a masked emissary of General Z, who appeared at every meeting.

One-half of the money stuck in the claws of the local leaders, and they kept their followers in good humor by providing free beer at the meetings, hot dogs, and hamburgers.

The ex-service men among them were pressed into commission as drill instructors. Their weapons consisted mainly of pick-handles for the rank and file, and revolvers for the officers. There was not a pistol permit in the outfit. They had reached a fair degree of precision in close-order drill, and were being instructed in the rudiments of street fighting *a la* Nazi. Every meeting was opened with the Star Spangled Banner and a very fancy oath in which they pledged allegiance to their country, their flag, their homes, their church, and General Z.

I almost neglected to say that in setting up their military organization they did not forget the spiritual side. Cardinals and dozens of bishops of assorted denomination had been offered commissions as Chaplain-Generals.

There had been tentative plans made to extend the organization to other cities. They had gone so far as to nominate and appoint recruiting officers who were to spread out through the country and act as walking delegates. Probably the only thing that stopped this plan from being put into effect was the greed of the leaders, who had not yet taken sufficient money to satisfy them. In another three months, they would have been going full tilt on a national basis.

"Who was this masked emissary of General Z?" Tonelli asked.

The Four-Square spokesmen swore they didn't know. Their meetings were held across the river at an abandoned amusement park which they had been able to rent for a trifling sum. The General's emissary always arrived in a car which was suspiciously like that used for official business by the late Commodore Ireton. In addition to being masked in a purple hood, this man also wore a long purple cloak which completely disguised his figure. He was of medium height, he had a resonant voice, and that was all they knew about him. The car was always stopped outside the park; and neither messenger nor chauffeur ever left the shelter of it. The chauffeur sat with his cap pulled over his eyes and his coat-collar turned up.

This Messenger had achieved his mysterious effect beautifully. When our informants spoke of him they bated their breath.

"Do you think this man was Commodore Ireton?" Tonelli asked.

One of the brightest of the group denied that.

"It couldn't have been Commodore Ireton, because the Messenger attended a meeting night before last, which was after the Commodore had been killed," he said.

"What else does this masked marvel do besides collect the dough?" Tonelli asked.

"He makes speeches and he delivers us the orders of General Z," was the answer.

"How do you know these orders come from General Z?" Tonelli demanded.

"Because the orders are always written, and signed. And in addition to that, they are sealed with purple sealing wax and imprinted with the Great Seal of the organization."

"Have you got any of these written orders?" Tonelli asked.

The answer was No. "The orders are always shown to the Council of Four, which is composed of the senior officers present at a meeting, and as soon as these officers have read and fully understood the orders, the orders are burned before us all by the council. The sergeant-at-arms then goes to the Messenger's car and reports the orders have been received, understood and been burned as may we all burn in Hell if they are not obeyed. The Messenger always waits for this report before he drives away. We are not allowed to have any written correspondence or records in the organization."

"That's a useful regulation," I commented. Tonelli agreed.

"What kind of orders do you get from General Z?" Tonelli asked.

"All kinds of orders," they answered. "Sometimes we are ordered not to patronize certain stores in town, or not to buy goods manufactured by certain companies. Sometimes we are told to buy from some certain people, and what to buy. Sometimes the orders are messages about national or local politics."

"Are you ever ordered to vote for certain men?" asked Tonelli.

"No," the answer was a little doubtful. "But usually we are told to vote against men who have said certain things or stand for certain things. That gives us a pretty clear idea of who we should vote for."

"You don't have to do much thinking for yourselves, do you?" Tonelli commented. Then he asked: "What other kind of orders do you get? Do they ever tell you to go out and beat somebody up?"

They were reluctant to answer that question. Tonelli had to do quite a lot of pounding to get the answer, but at last it came out. There was a secret branch of the Four-Square known as the Confidence Corps. Nobody knew who belonged to this elite group. Our informants denied to a man that they belonged, but it was admitted that there were undoubtedly several among the fifty-two which confronted us. The Confidence Corps carried out the instructions of General Z that were too dangerous or delicate for the ordinary rank and file. The regular membership knew of the existence of this Corps principally because it was constantly held over their heads as a threat. Each Four-Square member knew if he failed to obey orders, the Confidence Corps would take him in hand. He knew there were many of these CC men scattered through the membership. A man's bosom pal might be a CC and be relaying information to General Z and his Messenger.

"What do you call this bird in the purple night shirt?" Tonelli asked.

"He is called the Messenger. That's all," they said. "We have no other name for him."

"Seems to me," Tonelli said in his most engaging manner, "that you fellows would have been pretty curious about this messenger. Didn't anybody do any snoopin' around?"

After some hesitation one of the men answered:

"We were afraid to. One or two men who did were flogged. We found it was a good idea not to know too much about General Z and his Messenger."

"Do you think Commodore Ireton was General Z?" Tonelli asked.

They either could not, or would not, answer that question; and Tonelli didn't press it.

"How did you know members of your organization, out of the lodge and out of uniform?" Tonelli asked.

For answer one of the men pointed to the purple square of enamel he wore in his buttonhole.

"What, no secret signs?" said Tonelli incredulously.

The men looked foolishly from one to the other, and finally admitted they had a secret sign which was at once identification and signal of distress. It was simple: they merely placed the back of one hand, the right, in the palm of the left hand, at right angles. Apparently the louder the smack they made with the gesture, the greater was their need.

Tonelli motioned for me to follow him, and we left them in the bull pen. Out in the desk room of the station house a loud-voiced lawyer demanded immediate access to his clients of the Purple Shirt. The desk sergeant was making heavy weather of it. He looked up hopefully as Tonelli and I passed, but Tonelli jerked his head in faint negative gesture and with a slight downward motion of his hand managed to suggest that he wanted the shyster impeded and detained. The desk sergeant, red in the face, worried, turned wearily back to his task of combating the shoddy oratory of the lawyer.

Saying nothing, Tonelli shoved me into his car and stepped on the starter. Several groups of men lounged in the street near the station. They were quite unusually curious about our car, but Tonelli did not notice them.

"I'll bet you a ten-dollar hat," I offered, "I can guess the name of General Z's messenger in three guesses, and all three'll be the same name."

Tonelli said, "Well?"

"Izzie Jones," I guessed. "He could never resist that mask and purple nightgown."

Tonelli stepped a little harder on the gas. We sped downtown in heavy traffic, and at the entrance to the bridge Tonelli leaned out of the car and waved for a police radio car in which were two officers, to go ahead of us. They swept past, their siren going full blast, and we took the long bridge like a pair of tomcats on a high board fence, passing all the cars jammed in six abreast. Across the bridge Tonelli signaled for the escort to kill its siren and fall behind.

It was only a short run to the old recreation park where we tumbled out. Tonelli and the two officers gave the place a quick but thorough going over. In the center of the park stood an old building which had once been the pavilion for dancing, the restaurant and refreshment stand. It was heavily shuttered and boarded up. One of the doors was held by a flimsy lock which Tonelli demolished with one well-delivered kick. He took a flashlight from the pocket of his car, and entered followed by the two officers and myself. The place was empty, cold and damp, but there was ample evidence that it had been used exactly as the Four-Square members had described. On the raised platform, once the throne of the orchestra, was a table, and at each end of the table stumps of candles had guttered in their own grease.

Tonelli, flashing his light behind the table, had discovered a small cupboard in the wainscoting at the rear of the stage. This also he broke open. Inside was a neatly folded American flag, a gavel, and nothing more. These Tonelli took for evidence.

He tilted his hat forward and scratched his head.

"There must be a membership roster of this nutty outfit," he muttered. "I wonder where they keep it."

It was certainly not in that building. The place was bare and although we found refuse such as stale rolls with half-eaten frankfurters and a few thick glasses showing they had once held beer, and an empty keg, there was nothing of importance. Tonelli swore in disgust and disappointment. He gave orders to the radio patrol, and once again behind a screaming siren we sped across the bridge.

"I suppose," said Tonelli, his eyes intent on the roadway, "I'll have to get fifty-two search warrants issued and search all those goofs' houses."

"On what charge are you holding these men?" I asked. "How are you going to get search warrants?"

Tonelli frowned intently at the roadway. "Conspiracy," he said briefly.

"How much of this are you going to give to the papers?" I asked.

"As much as they ask for," he said. "If they don't ask for anything, they'll get nothing."

"And I used to think you were the newspaperman's friend," I commented.

We came to the end of the bridge, and Tonelli waved a hand dismissing our escort. The radio car drew up to its place at the curb, and its occupants lapsed into that semi-torpid alertness which the policeman habitually assumes when out of action.

"Where to now?" I asked Tonelli.

"Back to the station house," he answered. "I thought maybe I could put a fast one over on these boys. They didn't know they were going to be called in today, and I thought they might have left something important at their meeting place and not had a chance to hide it before I got there."

We swung off the main avenue and began zigzagging across town, taking advantage of the change in lights. Tonelli gauged them to the split second. We were halted only once by the red in the course of some thirty-five blocks, which is something for good drivers to try and duplicate.

The uptown street we moved along before we turned off into the side street where the station house stood, was badly lighted and narrow. Yet even in the bad light I could see a considerable crowd had gathered on the corner nearest to the police station. As we approached that corner, a sharp report rang out and a louder bang as our rear tire blew.

We were moving about fifty miles an hour. The car slewed and lurched, Tonelli fighting the wheel. The rear end swung dizzily, the car leaped diagonally across the street, skidded completely around in a half turn, and fetched up with a jarring crash against a stone stoop blocking the sidewalk. Tonelli was out on his feet with his gun in his hand, running back along our route as fast as he could tear. I saw a shadow dash out from the shelter of a porch halfway down the street, a revolver flashed, and Tonelli's gun answered.

The shadow did not stagger. It kept on and around the corner a block away. Tonelli raced that far, pulled up short, and walked back panting. As he approached the car where I still sat, he flipped open the chamber of his revolver and inserted a fresh cartridge for the one he had fired.

"You're a fine pal," he said. "You can run faster than me. Why didn't you help me run that guy down?"

"Fine pal yourself," I said back. "If you expect me to leave the shelter of a nice all-metal car just for the pleasure of dodging hot lead without any to throw back, you're coo-coo."

He bent over to examine the damage to the car. The left front fender and the running board was crumpled, and the wire wheel on the left rear was bent and useless. It was the tire on that wheel our shadowy friend had shot out from under us.

I crawled out and stood beside him, but he was no longer intent on the car. Slowly, ominously, the crowd from the corner was edging down the street toward us.

"Looks like we've got a reception committee," I remarked.

"Somebody must have clapped his hands together and they thought it was the distress signal," Tonelli said grimly.

"You must come from an awful tough neighborhood," I said, "if handclapping sounds like pistol shots and tire blowouts."

"Sure, it was a tough neighborhood," Tonelli admitted. "But I never learned any tough ways myself. My mother always taught me to be a gentleman."

"Was it your pappy who taught you always to reload as soon as you've fired a shot?" I asked.

"Naw, my pop was afraid of guns." As he spoke Tonelli put away his revolver. I noticed he did not replace it in its holster. He slipped it into his right coat pocket, where it would be handy.

10

"IT LOOKS TO ME," Tonelli spoke with an accented if casual deliberation, "as if we're in for a few ructions."

I achieved a hollow laugh. "That will be a novelty, won't it. I haven't *had* any ructions since I've been here."

Tonelli looked at me sharply. "Got your belly full already?" he queried.

"Up to my eyeteeth," I said, and then we were on the fringe of the crowd. There was that about the look of them which was unappetizing. They were glum. No conversation, none of the cheery side remarks, not even the gruffness and brusquerie that is present in a normal crowd. Once I saw the beginning of a lynch mob in the deep South, and this assemblage had the same sullen backwash and undercurrent.

Literally, this mob had fringes. So literally it was not entirely accidental.

I said to Tonelli, "Looks to me like they posted outguards."

"That's right," he said. "These guys we're coming to now are the lookouts. Whoever's handling this knows his stuff. All the exits to this street are blocked. They knew we were coming four or five blocks before we arrived, and were ready for us."

I suggested, "And the pleasant lad with the gun who wrecked us so neatly, was he the chairman of the reception committee?"

"That's right," said Tonelli.

We were coming close to the corner, and the five or six men who were lounging there moved into a loose line across the sidewalk. I may not have mentioned it before, but my friend Lieutenant Tonelli is six feet two inches tall. He weighs 230 pounds, and there's not an ounce of fat on him. His hands are like something you buy in a butcher shop, with all the bones left in. And his neck is the despair of haberdashers. Without realizing he was crowding me, he stepped slightly to the right and in front of me, and sauntered toward the space between the two men who were blocking the center of the sidewalk, flanked by their friends. It was a space that did scant justice to Tonelli's beam. He, however, considered it ample. Although his pace did not accelerate, when he reached that small opening he was moving with purpose. The two men who boxed him in were not infantile in their proportions, but when he struck they spun in opposite directions as if set on pivots. I walked through like a best man behind the bridegroom, and got about as much attention from the onlookers.

There was a kind of inarticulate sound which might be called snarl, from the men Tonelli had shouldered aside; I could feel the goosepimples gallivant around my vertebrae. Tonelli did not pause, did not go faster, gave no sign he was aware of any difficulty. We approached the more solid main body lumped between us and the door of the police station, almost side by side.

Over the heads of the men between us and the comparative safety of the double green lights, I could see two patrolmen standing in front of the station door with riot clubs at the ready. The whole building was lighted brilliantly. Evidently men off duty were not snoozing in the bunkrooms upstairs, nor were they playing their eternal pinochle game. I wondered how many reserves there were in this precinct, and how many of them were present, and ready for the battle, and I hoped they liked the prospect better than I did.

To my surprise, the men we were approaching in that outwardly solid mass gave back, inch by inch, as Tonelli went forward. There may have been one or two who knew him by sight and reputation, in which case no wonder they dodged the issue as long as possible.

Then began the hum. That buzz which comes out of the heart of an angry and sullen crowd. No man seemed to be speaking, but the hum rose a little higher each step we advanced, higher and higher, until it began to take shape in words. Not the chanted slogans of peaceful picketers, but disjointed, disconnected words and phrases threatening us by their delirious pitch and cadence rather than their content.

Then—and it was almost a shock—there was a hard, fast line of solid humanity blocking our passage. The yielding mass stood firm. From behind us men on the fringes closed in so near we could feel the proverbial hot breath on our necks. Very likely I've been much nearer to death then I was at that moment but I have never been so keenly aware of it.

Tonelli spoke. "Well, what is this?" he said with all the official belligerence of the trained cop. "Break this up. Move aside, there. I'm a headquarters man. I've got to get into that station house."

Something whizzed past Tonelli's shoulder and so close to my head I felt the air disturbance of its passage, and flinched.

Tonelli went into action.

Those two enormous hands shot out shoulder high for all the world like twins of the clamshell bucket at the end of a dredging beam. Both hands dropped on the shoulders of a smallish man in front of him. The man was lifted off his feet and hurled backwards into the faces of the crowd. His feet must have been six inches off the ground and he struck first with his shoulders.

It was a complete surprise, and Tonelli followed it instantly. He moved into the space left by the man he had plucked up by the roots, and grasped the astonished necks of the two next men in the ranks behind, pulling their heads together with a crack that put them both out of action for quite a time.

Once more I was in the position of strolling down a broad corridor only this time I was behind some legendary animal. That second crack released the spell. There was no longer a feeling of serried packed ranks of men. The street was suddenly full of writhing, shouting units.

That was something I understood a little better. The old circus tactics in a mob fight can never be improved upon. The thing to do—and I did it, at the expense of skinned knuckles and sore muscles—is to hit, anybody, anywhere, but keep on hitting and never smack the same baby twice. I forgot my sore left arm. Forgot to be scared. Nobody can fight a hundred men, but a lad who is fairly fast on his feet can make a good big crowd know they've been in a fight, providing they're not permitted to gang up simultaneously, and as long as he never attempts to slug it out with one man.

Somehow, as much engaged and interested as I was in my own affairs, I had still time to sense rather than observe the magnificent smoothness of Pete. He looked as awkward as a Kodiak bear when he was in repose, but in his element he was beautiful. Those tremendous meat axes that hung at the ends of his arms clipped and punched and jabbed. He threw his weight in exactly the right direction, at exactly the right time. He slugged, shoved, or flung aside the man directly in front of him, and always there was another man to take the place of those who staggered aside. Actually my job resolved itself to mopping up in his wake.

It is my firm belief that if Tonelli's actual steps from the corner of the street to the station house door were counted, it would be found they were identical with the number of steps he would have taken had he been strolling along a deserted pavement.

The carnage was terrific. It took perhaps forty-five seconds to traverse the short distance we had to go before we reached the space that was being cleared for us in front of the station by the clubs of the police reserves who came surging from the door as the shouting began. Yet that time seemed a year, or a second. It had ceased to be time, and had become a swirl of hot and bloody action.

On the top step I yanked out my handkerchief and blew my nose, and was surprised to find that it was sore and that my handkerchief was filled with blood. Tonelli hadn't a scratch on him. He looked at me and laughed.

"How about it, kid?" he questioned. "Did you dish out as much as you took?"

That colossal Wop had actually had a good time—and, in thinking it over, so had I.

Inside the station, the shyster lawyer was still ramping up and down in front of the desk, the desk sergeant was still red in the face, and the fifty-two boys of the Four-Square Americans were still securely locked in the pen. Outside, the crowd, deprived of its prey—which is to say, Tonelli and me—was giving vent to its displeasure in a raucous manner that would do justice to Times Square at the stroke of midnight, January 1. The captain commanding the precinct came through the door mopping his superheated brow, with a riot stick dangling on its thong from his wrist. At that moment I noticed he favored a cypress stick. Some cops like mahogany, and a few even consider walnut the best. A real workman, however, sticks to cypress. It has such a nice, convincing ring when it connects.

"What do you think?" the captain said to Tonelli. "Shall I cut loose the boys and try to clear them out, or shall I turn in a riot call?"

Tonelli stepped to the door and surveyed the mob critically. He was as much listening as he was looking, gauging their temper as well as size. But I doubt if he knew that. He turned to the captain and said:

"You could drive a wedge into 'em, with this force you've got here. But you couldn't scatter them. I want to get these prisoners down to the city jail anyhow; I'll call up headquarters and have them send up a couple of loads of men. When we hear 'em coming we can start in from the middle here and the downtown boys can close in from both sides. I'd like to pick up forty or fifty of those lads out there. I might be able to get something from them if I put them in the sweatbox." As calm and businesslike as a couple of certified public accountants talking over the exemptions in Mr. Rockefeller's income tax.

The shyster lawyer rose to tremendous heights of frenzied rhetoric as Tonelli walked calmly into the captain's office and got on the telephone. He explained what he wanted, how he wanted the men disposed, how many men he wanted arrested from the mob, and in three minutes was back again, at rest, peaceful.

Nothing to do but to wait. I went into the toilet with a first-aid kit, stoppered up my bleeding nose, and tried to clean some of the blood from my coat lapel and tie. My knuckles were feeling a little the worse for wear by then too, and I splashed them liberally with mercurochrome, which added to the incarnadined color scheme.

Under Tonelli's instructions, the fifty-two captives were lined up in the bull pen and neatly clipped together in pairs with handcuffs. Also under his instructions, the converging patrol wagons and squad cars kept their sirens quiet until they were nearly at the point of contact, and swooped from four directions at once. Then sirens filled the air. Sound and brass buttons came from all points of the compass, striking confusion and terror into the heart of every would-be rescuer in the crowd outside. Tonelli posted himself on the steps with the reserve section behind him, searching the crowd with his eyes. As it began to break into groups, to rush in all directions seeking a loophole of escape from the oncoming riot squads, Tonelli dashed into the midst of the turmoil and came back dragging a pale, rat-like man by the collar. He opened the station house door with his left hand, and with his right flung the captive halfway across the floor.

The man struck on his hands and knees and slid, and before he completely lost motion or could get to his feet, Tonelli was standing over him.

"Talk, and talk fast," the Lieutenant ordered.

The man whined.

Tonelli stooped, wrenched him to his feet, and threatened him with a clenched fist.

"Talk fast," he ordered venomously, "or I'll let you have it."

"What—what do you want me to say?" the man whined.

"You brought this crowd here, didn't you?" Tonelli stated.

The man shook his head.

Tonelli rattled him like a burlesque queen with a grass skirt.

"Don't lie. Spit it out. You brought these men here, didn't you."

"No, sir," the man quavered.

"You had something to do with it," Tonelli insisted.

"I only brought the orders," the fellow was close to tears.

"What orders, from whom?" Tonelli shook him like a second-hand motorcycle sidecar.

"Orders from The Messenger," the man said.

"Who is The Messenger?" Tonelli demanded.

"I don't know," the man sobbed.

"Where did you see him?" Tonelli asked.

"I met him on the corner," the man was openly crying now. "He came driving up in his car."

"What's his car number?" Tonelli roared.

"I don't know. I didn't see. It was covered with dust. Honest, mister, the license plates was covered with dust."

Tonelli rattled him again, shaking the tears from his face in a shower.

"How did you know what corner to meet him on?"

"He called me up, at my house," the rat sobbed. "Honest he did, mister. He called me up and told me where to be, and when. I was scared not to go. You don't know these guys. If I didn't go, they might bump me off."

"What did his face look like?" Tonelli questioned.

"I couldn't see his face. He kept back in the car, and besides, he had his mask on."

"What was the message he gave you? What were the orders you brought?"

The rat answered as if it were a matter of course. "He told me to call the emergency mobilization number, and when I got hold of the chief of the Confidence Corps, I was to tell him to concentrate his men in front of this station house, and stand by to rescue our brothers that was arrested."

"What is this mobilization thing?" Tonelli demanded.

"Why," said the man, still with that matter-of-fact manner, "everybody in the organization has his post assigned for mobilization. All we got to do is to obey the order when it comes, either by messenger or by telephone. Every Four-Square American has got to have a telephone number where he can be reached. The Confidence Corps attends to all that. To turn in a special or a general aid or mobilization call you dial MU 7654 and tell the man who answers what you want, and where you got your orders."

Tonelli shook him loose in a gesture that spun him up against the wall.

"Put irons on that guy," he ordered, and strode back out into the street, with me trailing faithfully. I had concluded the safest spot in town was directly behind Pete's broad shoulders.

The squad cars and the patrols had arrived at the ends of the street. The middle of the block was practically deserted, and there was a fine shindy going on at both corners. The light was failing, and the action obscured in a blur of shadows. I wished George Bellows could be alive and standing with me at my point of vantage. What a dry-point he could have made of that scene, and how he would have loved it.

The reserves from the station house split into two sections, one headed by the precinct lieutenant and Tonelli, and the other by the precinct captain. They bore down on both rears of the split mob of rioters in flying wedges. Nightsticks rang like wedding bells.

Concerted team work did the job. The police allowed the great majority of the crowd to trickle through their lines, handing out to each a passing kiss with a club. When the clamor of battle had subsided, there were only fourteen men for the ambulances to cart away, and only two of these were policemen. It was a triumph of artistry over mere brute strength.

That old slogan "You Can't Win!" had added poignancy and significance to the lads who had begun this party and couldn't quite finish it. Eighty-one prisoners in all were delivered at the city jail in good order. The original fifty-two, Tonelli's rat-like personal captive, and the rest picked up by the police reinforcements as per instructions from the Lieutenant.

In the jailer's office Tonelli and I munched ham and egg sandwiches and washed them down with black coffee from the lunch wagon across the street, while the tedious formality of booking this bumper haul was completed.

With the yolk of an underdone egg oozing down the side of my chin, I mumbled to Tonelli over and between a bit of sandwich: "Where did you get the list you read out in the theatre?"

"Wipe your chin," Tonelli admonished. "What do you think we been doing behind the locked doors of Commodore Ireton's office all this time?"

"Oh, Lieutenant!" I simpered. "Don't ask me what policemen do behind locked doors."

Tonelli took another bite of his sandwich. "There was a lot of interesting things in that office," he confided. "In one steel cabinet every drawer held a treasure. If you're a good boy and live long enough I'll tell you about some of the things we found. But I'm telling you now, you won't keep your health and beauty if you go around insulting cops."

"Was Four-Square's roster in the locked cabinet?" I ignored his warning.

Tonelli emphasized his remarks with a half-eaten cruller. "No. But there was everything else you ever heard about in the cabinet.

There was a complete list of the officers, their ranks, their duties. It even gave the amount of money each one was supposed to kick through with every week."

"The Commodore must have been making a sweet thing out of it," I suggested.

"No," Tonelli was very thoughtful. "I don't think he got much of the dough. We've checked up on his bank account, and he hasn't got much cash on hand—no more than he would have from his salary. We've combed every safe deposit in the town, and there isn't a lockbox anywhere in his name, and none of the guards or bank officials can remember a man of his description."

"Probably the lockbox was in Sarah Hirzner's name," I prompted. "Maybe *she* had a bank account too."

Tonelli snatched the last cruller.

"You think of everything, don't you. Well, listen, kid: she didn't have any dough in her bank account except for a few hard-earned dollars in her savings bank. She didn't have any lockbox either."

"Well, my bucko," I covered my confusion, "you got the name of the mysterious guy in the purple nightshirt didn't you? The Messenger?"

Tonelli gulped the last of his cruller.

"You're picking all the wrong numbers," he told me. "Every other guy in the organization was named, except The Messenger—who was carried on the rolls just like that—and General Z, who was also carried on the rolls just like that."

"Was Commodore Ireton's name on the roll?" I asked.

"Yes," said Tonelli. "He was Lieutenant General, in command of this district."

"Then," I said, "Ireton couldn't have been General Z."

Tonelli rose and yawned. "Yeah," he said, "we figured that out too."

A sergeant came in to report that the prisoners were all booked, had been given preliminary examinations, and were awaiting the Lieutenant's disposal. Tonelli yawned again.

"Lock 'em up," he directed. "Let 'em stew in their own juice to-night. They'll be a lot softer in the morning. And tell the Doc not to be too liberal with handing out the arnica and the bandages. Let 'em ache. That'll help soften them up too."

The sergeant started out of the room. Tonelli's voice halted him at the door.

"Oh, yeah, one more thing, Sergeant. Tell the chief turnkey to keep the lights in the cell block burning bright all night. I don't want these mugs to get too much rest."

He yawned for the third time, and stretched mightily. A slight grimace obscured his ugly but pleasant Italian map. "Jeest," he said, "I gotta begin to take a little workout in the gym every day. I'm gettin' fat. Exercise like this gets me all stiffened up."

"Now listen, Tonelli," I said, "I'm too sore and tired to sleep. You sit right down here and let's go over this case. I want to know what *you* know. What have you found out? What clues have you got? Have you any idea who did these murders? And if you haven't, when are you going to have an idea?"

"If you gotta talk," he said wearily, "come on, let's go across the street to the Greek's and have another cup of java. I've gotta have something to keep me awake. Jeest, they put the rest of the force on a three platoon system, but me—I don't ever get to bed. My wife thinks she's married to a travelin' man."

To sweeten him up I said, "How's your boy doing in law school these days?"

His face lighted with the pride that always shone in it when he spoke of Tonelli, Junior. "Say," he bragged, "that kid's all right. I dunno where he gets all the brains, but he's just eatin' up that school thing. He's gonna graduate next spring."

I said, "That's fine. You going to go and see him graduate?"

Tonelli got suspicious.

"Hey," he jibed, "what is this, the old mullarkey? Are you trying to butter me?"

"Certainly not," I denied. "I like that kid of yours. As you say, I don't know where he gets all the brains; but that's something I'll let *you* fight out with the Mrs."

Tonelli made a playful pass at me, and having seen one or two of those playful passes land that evening, I ducked and sidestepped and gave him plenty of leeway.

The sergeant who had come in to report on the prisoners stuck his head in the door. "Okay, Lieut," he reported. "We did everything like you said. And say Lieut, you're wanted on the telephone."

Tonelli took up the receiver and said, "Well?" He frowned. "Yes, Bill. What is it—When did you pick him up?—What makes you think so?—Was that all?—Was there any description on the card?—Then you don't know whether it's his card or not.—I guess maybe I'd better come down. I'll be down there pretty soon. Don't let him get away.—Yeah, that's right; keep him on ice for me."

"That was the morgue," said Tonelli, hanging up. "The police launch picked up a floater in the river a little while ago. They're holding him for me to have a look at. Wanna come along?"

I said, "No, thanks. I've seen 'em when they come in from the river like that. They're not pretty."

"You better change your mind," Tonelli said, "and come along with me. This might be a friend of yours."

"My friends don't go swimming in this weather," I said.

"What about Mr. Bennington Graeme?" Tonelli reminded me. "He took a swim for himself, didn't he?"

"If we had an efficient police department in this city," I snapped, "there wouldn't be these nasty incidents."

"Forget it," said Tonelli. "Let's go down to the cold storage house."

There was no reason why I should go, I didn't want to go, dead men make me sick; but—I tagged along out to the car.

11

OUT AT THE CURB there was a brand new department Ford waiting for us, and as we drove down the street we passed a wrecking car towing in what was left of the machine Tonelli had driven earlier in the evening, and which we had wrecked on the way back from our visit to the Four-Square Americans' trysting place.

"Where can we get a slug of liquor?" I asked Tonelli. "My throat feels like a nutmeg grater."

He said, "I know a place down the street a ways. We'll stop in and get you a pint. You can carry it on your hip. You'll probably need it when we get to the cold meat house."

"Nice law-abiding citizen you are," I rebuked him. "Encouraging blind tigers to break the city ordinances by selling liquor after mid-night."

"How else is a thirsty guy going to get the stuff?" Tonelli said in a matter-of-fact tone. "This is a useful place. The lug that runs it is one of our best stoolies."

The liquor was just right. If it had been a little worse, I couldn't have drunk it; if it had been any better, the guy that sold it couldn't have afforded to do business. I comforted myself with little swigs while we rounded the gas-house district onto the docks and finally pulled up outside of that unattractive building in which the city beds down its forgotten dead.

Tonelli's muscles might ache, but he hopped out of the car with the same spry alacrity with which he had approached battle earlier in the evening. I decided to wait in the hall while he went into the vault and looked over his find. He was gone a considerable time, and when he came back he took me into the Chief Toxicologist's office, and we sat on opposite sides of that official's desk. From a large envelope he spread a few things on the desk. All of the articles were dry, but were in a pulpy and wrinkled state which showed they had been long in the water. There was a leather belt, with a cheap imitation-silver buckle mounted with the initial M. Clipped to the remains of a card case, the seams of which had come unglued, were several blurred cards and scraps of paper. One of these scraps of paper was a WPA pay-identification slip, bearing the name of John O. Martin, and his serial number, which was partially effaced by the action of the water.

"Do you know anybody by the name of John O. Martin?" Tonelli asked me.

I was happy to report I had no such friend.

The other papers were such trivia as are to be found in any man's card case. There was what looked as if it might have been a poem clipped from a newspaper, but the water had made it illegible. There was a torn sheet of letter paper with an inky blurred address. There was an accident insurance identification card, and we could make out enough of it to see that the policy had lapsed by five years. There was no driver's license, and no motor-car registration. None of the cards or papers gave any clue to the physical description of the man to whom the card case had belonged. The other objects in the pile on the desk were the usual flotsam, the knick-knacks a man carried in his pocket. A bunch of keys, a lucky penny set in the middle of an aluminum disc. A brace of handkerchiefs which must have been soiled even before the river had completed the job. A tie clip, a pair of cheap cufflinks. It was a pitiful array, cheap and trivial. The belongings of a floater even before he had been confided to the river.

"This guy didn't have very much," Tonelli spoke. "But what he had was not too gaudy. Imitation black seal pocketbook. Imitation silver buckle. Tie clip and cufflinks imitation gold."

"Quite the imitation gentleman," I cracked.

"He was in there trying, I guess. Like us all," said Tonelli.

He shoveled things back into the envelope, after making some notes in his memorandum book, and said, "Sorry, kid, you better take another good long swig at that bottle. I want you to come in and look at the corpse and tell me if you've ever seen the fellow before. He's not bad, his face is just a little puffed up."

I dragged along after him, took a real swig just before the door opened, took a quick look at the corpse on the slab, pelted as hard as I could back to the door, and snatched another quick swig.

"Some fresh air will fix you all right," Tonelli said at my elbow.

In the car the liquor began to take a grip. In a minute or so I was enough interested in life to ask where we were going, for Tonelli had headed into the jungle along the docks.

For answer he slipped the car through a pier gate and we drove slowly along, our headlights switched on full. The beams of light rested on the familiar outlines of the harbor police patrol boat.

Tonelli set the brakes, hopped down and called, "Hey, Donald! Are you aboard?"

From the tiny bridge deck of the boat came an answering call. "Surest thing you know. Come aboard, Pete. Make yourself at home."

In the crowded saloon we faced Marine Sergeant Donald Mac-Intosh, who was said to know every ripple in the river by its maiden name.

"We need some dope on that floater your boys picked up this afternoon," Tonelli began.

"Anything, anytime, for you, Pete. You know me," said the water-man.

"Where did you find him?" Pete asked.

"He was about two hundred yards off the west shore, floating along in the rip tide. You know that spot, Pete. It's just opposite the railroad freight shops."

"You find a lot of 'em there, don't you, Donald?"

"Yes," said Donald. "But that doesn't mean that they jumped in there."

Tonelli said dryly, "If this fellow jumped, he was quite a lad. The autopsy shows he was dead before he was dumped in the water. There's no water in his lungs."

"I noticed that. Somebody's tapped him over the head," the Marine Sergeant agreed with the diagnosis. Tonelli included me in the conversation.

"Donald here," he told me, "knows more about drowned stiffs than all the medical examiners and coroners put together. He's been fishing 'em out of the river for twenty years, and he can tell you whether they were drowned or not, and from where he picked them up he can tell you where they went in. He can almost tell if they jumped, were pushed, or thrown."

"Do you mean to say," I asked, going through the motions of being astonished, "the Sergeant can tell us where this particular body was thrown into the river?"

The grizzled old harborman grinned proudly.

"I think I can," he boasted. "You know, the old river," he said as pridefully as one would speak of his country estate, "is a pretty good old gal. She's got regular habits. She never disappoints you. She's always on time. Her currents and tides are the same, year in and year out, if you make due allowance for the sun and the moon."

"Makes it very handy, too," Tonelli put in. "A lot of murders have been solved that way."

"These murderers ain't got much imagination," the Marine sergeant said, "when they've got to get rid of a body, the first and the last thing they think of is to dump it in the river. Sometimes they cut 'em up, and then we just find a bundle with arms or legs in it, or something. Sometimes they put weights on 'em, and then we don't find 'em unless the weights slip. I remember once we found one arm and one leg of the same body floatin' off the Point. Two or three days later some boys swimming off the mud flats towed in a bundle with the other arm and the other leg. But we never did get that head."

I murmured faintly, "That's too bad."

"I remember that case," said Tonelli. "The position of those parts of bodies told Donald here a whole lot. He figured out the three bundles had been dropped overboard at different times of the day, and at different spots, by somebody on the ferryboat. Then we had to do a lot of asking around. I had four men riding the ferries every trip. I guess we questioned every commuter between town and the West Shore. Finally we found a fellow who remembered a man and a woman carrying a heavy bundle on board the boat. He saw 'em when they got off, and they didn't have the bundle. We checked up on the description, and caught the murderers."

"What about this immediate and present body?" I put in, hoping to stave off some more gruesome details.

The Marine Sergeant went up to the charthouse, and came back with a chart of the river which showed figures on the speed and direction of the currents. With a horny fingernail and a pair of dividers he began to trace out the course of the body's journeys.

"Now," he said, "we found the body just here. The current runs there pretty fast, at a speed of about three miles an hour. From the looks of it the body had been in the water about eleven hours."

"The doctor who made the post-mortem said between eleven and twelve," Tonelli murmured. He said to me in an aside Donald could hear, "I told you Donald knew his stuff."

The sergeant was pleased.

"If the current at this point," he continued his lecture, "is running at three miles an hour, and the body has been in the water for eleven hours—or maybe twelve—that means it's been carried thirty-three miles. But look here: you see how this current is deflected here? It hits the Hook and gets a kind of swirl. Now you trace across the current backwards, and you find it leads right into that swirl. I've known things to stay floatin' round and round off the Hook for eight or nine hours. They come into the edge of the circle, and they work their way through to the middle and out to the opposite edge. Then the straight sweep of the current gets 'em again, and they're carried on to the Point where we picked up this body. There's a kind of little dead spot there, and a lot of the harbor flotsam collects. It's one of the places we always look for bodies on our three regular daily patrols."

He was manipulating the dividers as he talked, stepping off lengths of three miles on the chart.

"Now you see," he went on, "where we picked up the body it's just a little bit over three miles from the swirl of the Hook. That means it took the body an hour to get from the place where we found it to the Hook. You understand, I'm talking backwards. I mean it took an hour for the body to get from the Hook to the place where we found it."

He paused to see we were following him closely.

"Now we have to allow nine hours—well, make it eight—for the body to stay in the swirl off the Hook. That makes nine hours our body's been in the water now."

"Make it your body," I murmured. "I don't want any part of it."

"The current don't run quite so fast above the swirl—say two and a half miles an hour. Now we know the body's been in the water for nine hours up to the point we traced it, and we know it's been in the water eleven or twelve hours altogether. That means it's been travelling, at the rate of the current above the swirl, five or six miles."

"On the east or west side of the river?" Tonelli asked.

"Oh, on the west side," the sergeant spoke very positively. With the points of his calipers he measured off five miles on the chart scale, placed one point at the edge of the swirl and swung the other around. It came to rest on the west bank of the river, just above the bridge.

Tonelli leaned over eagerly, almost sniffing the map.

"Look," his finger jabbed the chart, beside the caliper point. "What do you think of that?"

"What?" I asked.

"That," Tonelli repeated. "That spot right there is the old amusement park, where our friends the Purple Shirts had their meetings. Looks pretty clear to me. I think if we can get hold of the leaders of the Confidence Corps, they can tell us a great deal about the death of this young man."

Old Donald smiled with infinite self-satisfaction.

"Is this all you want?"

"I think that's all," Tonelli said. "We landlubbers oughta be able to figure out the rest of this, now that you've done the important part of the work."

"Don't try to kid the old man," Donald said as he rolled up the chart. But he was pleased and kidded just the same.

We clambered over the side of the tug, but Tonelli did not immediately get back into the car. He moved along to the pierhead and stood there with the dawn wind ruffling the skirts of his coat, looking out into the river mists. I joined him, and with me there beside him he began thinking aloud.

"Let's see what we've got. First, there's a riot at the Administration Building. Now was that an accident, or did somebody deliberately plan it?"

"A woman fainted," I said. "That began it. It didn't look like a planned riot to me."

"Easy enough for a woman to fake a faint," Tonelli went on, "but I agree with you. The fight looked pretty natural to me. Those people had been standing there a long while. The sit-down strikers were worn out and with their nerves on edge. It only took something like that woman's keeling over to start them all raving. Well, that doesn't get us very far."

"Where are you trying to get?" I asked.

"If somebody had planned that riot," Tonelli explained, "it would be easier to put the finger on him. Or her. There are a limited number of people who have a close enough in with the project workers to launch them on a planned, pre-arranged riot. If it was an accident, anybody might have taken advantage of the confusion. Anybody who didn't like the Commodore, and who had been waiting a chance, could have walked in and killed him."

"Don't forget our little reconstructions," I reminded him. "The person who killed the Commodore was someone who knew him well enough to be able easily to take advantage of his opportunity."

Tonelli sighed. "That narrows it down a little, but not enough to make it simple. Now what do we get next? The Commodore's secretary gets bumped off. Again it is by somebody who must have known her well, because he knew how to get into her apartment by the back way, and he knew his way around in the interior of her apartment. If he didn't know her well he'd been watching her long enough to know her habits, but that's unlikely. If he'd been watching it would have been with a purpose. That purpose would be robbery. There was opportunity to get the paper before the Commodore's death and without killing the girl. Therefore the girl was killed to keep her from naming somebody she knew."

"How you do run on with your deductions," I jibed.

"The gal was killed in bed," said Tonelli. "She was killed as she lay there dozing. Doped by the doctor."

"Do you mean to say you suspect the doctor had some hand in this?" I asked.

"Hell no," said Tonelli. "The gal was hysterical. She was on the edge of a nervous crackup. The doctor gave her a sedative to quiet her nerves. It may be the man who committed the murder knew that."

"Why do you say it's a man?" I asked.

"I don't say it," said Tonelli, "but I guess it is. Ladies don't go in for stranglings and hitting people over the head. It's more a lady's style to poison, to stab, or to shoot. The ladies don't use their bare hands very much in murders. They use their fingernails in their own little private fights. They pull hair and kick. But that's all in good fun. When they get serious, they get deadly and they take no chances on missing."

"Then you think the same person killed both the Commodore and Sarah Hirzner?" I asked.

"Sure," said Tonelli, "don't you?"

"It occurred to me," I suggested, "that there were a couple of people who might have had a grudge against Hirzner personally. Any number of people. Take Jaze, for example. I don't think she did it, but she wouldn't be the first daughter that was jealous of her father. And Sarah Hirzner may have had a boy friend who wouldn't think much of the Commodore's pajamas being in her room. Not only that, but a girl who has to be the watchdog in a big executive's office irritates somebody a dozen times a day. A dozen times an hour. There are a lot of nuts in the WPA. That's inevitable. Many of the people who are working on the program aren't employable anywhere else. There isn't a day passes that the medico doesn't send some worker to the psychopathic ward at the City Hospital for observation. Sarah Hirzner may have kept one of these nuts from seeing the administrator. Said screwball may have been watching for a chance to take a crack at the girl."

"You save all that guff," said Tonelli, "and write it up for a Sunday feature after the case is over. When you get going good, you'll be able to prove we sent the wrong guy to the gallows. That is, if we catch the guy."

I said, "All right, wise cop. Go ahead with your case."

Tonelli resumed quietly where he left off.

"One of the objectives of the murderer of Sarah Hirzner was robbery. Don't forget that a paper was taken out of her secretary, and was taken out within a few minutes of her death—either before or after. Doesn't much matter which. The absence of dust in the space where the paper lay proves that to my satisfaction."

"You say paper, *now*," I said. "When we found that vacant space you thought it was a card. A five by seven record card like the Government uses. Couldn't that card have been one like that Van Gelder showed me? The one that had my life history on it?"

"I told you the other day," Tonelli reminded me, "we had made a mistake about the size of that space. My experts measured it, and it measured 6¼ by 8 inches, not 5 by 7."

"So what?" I said. "How does that prove it's a paper?"

"It doesn't prove it exactly," Tonelli admitted, "but a legal size sheet folded in half measures 6¼ by 8. Until we find something better, we'll call it a legal document."

"What kind of a legal document would Sarah Hirzner have that anybody would murder her for?" I asked.

"The document was Commodore Ireton's, the way I have it doped out," said Tonelli. "He had it in Sarah Hirzner's apartment for safe-keeping."

"Why would he put it there? With all the lock-boxes and filing cabinets in his office?" I demanded.

Tonelli thought.

"Why would he?" he asked in return. "The papers in his office, in the locked files, all had to do with his job, or the Four-Square Americans. He didn't have any personal papers there at all. His personal papers were in his own library at home."

"What do you think this paper was, the Commodore's will?" I asked. "If that's the case, you're building up a pretty strong body of circumstantial evidence against Jaze."

"All legal documents aren't wills," Tonelli said dryly. "Might have been a deed, might even have been a transcript of a pardon. There are thousands of legal documents the Commodore might have had, and in which he might have been personally interested."

"Granting this was a legal document, contents unknown," I goaded him on, "where does that get us?"

"That gets us a motive for the murder, and a logical sequence," Tonelli explained kindly. "Somebody was gunning for the Commodore. He took advantage of the riot to kill the Commodore. He gave a quick look around the office to find the paper he wanted, and it wasn't there. Then as soon as he got a chance, he went to Sarah Hirzner's apartment looking for the same paper. He went into Hirzner's bedroom, she woke up from her doze enough to recognize him, and he let her have it. He then got the paper and left the apartment."

"How does that link up with the Four-Square Americans and what has the third murder to do with it?"

"That's what we're going to find out," said Tonelli. "The first thing to do is to get hold of somebody in the WPA who knows a lot of the people, and can identify that corpse. We'll say, as a beginning, that the identification card he carries is his own."

"If it is, that's easy," I said. "We can get into the personnel office as soon as it opens, and check the files."

Tonelli drove me back to the hotel, I got a couple of hours of sleep, got into some fresh clothes, and turned up at the office a little before nine. It *would* be that morning the file clerk in the personnel office selected to be a half hour late; but I had plenty of work to do in the interval. Tonelli waited right there in the Personnel Division while I went to my own desk. Ten minutes after the file clerk came in, Tonelli was in my office with a record card. John O. Martin, according to the WPA, was a timekeeper on one of the engineering projects, a sewer job being finished up in connection with the Parks Department. We got the job location, and went out to interview the foreman.

All the workers rested on their picks and shovels and enjoyed the diversion our visit created. The foreman was most courteous and helpful, and inordinately long winded and diplomatic. We jolted him down to reality quick.

"John O. Martin," he said. "Sure, I know Johnny. Would you like to speak to him?"

Tonelli and I exchanged sour looks.

"Sure," said Tonelli. "Trot him out."

Johnny was towheaded and dumb, and very much alive.

"Let me see your identification slip," I ordered.

He made a motion toward his hip pocket, and grinned stupidly.

"I ain't got it," he confessed. "I lost it a coupla days ago. I lost my pocketbook and my keys and everything that was in my pockets. You see," he explained eagerly, "I was going to a dance down on the South Side. It wasn't exactly a dance, it was a kind of a party. We don't get off here till five o'clock, and it takes over an hour to get down there from here by the busses and street cars. I knew I wouldn't have time to go home and change my clothes so I wore my best suit to work, and carried my old pants in a bundle. I changed my pants over there in the tool shed, and left everything but my money in my pants pocket. Some guy got in there and stole it all. Jeest, it's a lucky thing there wasn't any money in there."

"It's lucky they didn't take the pants," said Tonelli.

"Ain't it?" The idea struck Johnny. "I guess I was lucky at that."

"Maybe you won't be so lucky when the paymaster comes around," I suggested. "How are you going to get paid without your identification slip?"

Johnny grinned.

"Ah, that's easy," he boasted. "I know the paymaster. He's an old buddy of mine."

I called the foreman.

"How many men on this project are being paid without showing their identification slips?" I demanded.

"None," the foreman insisted stoutly.

I pointed to Johnny.

"Send that lug downtown to get another identification slip," I said. "If I hear of anybody else on this project, or any other project, without a slip, the boss in charge of the project is going to get fired."

When we left, the picks and shovels were rising and falling at a high rate of speed, and dirt was being moved from that sewer excavation a lot faster than it had when we made our visit.

"Now what?" I asked Tonelli, as we went back to the Administration Building.

"Now," he said grimly, "I've got to get to work. We can't even be sure this fellow we pulled out of the river *is* a WPA employee; but we'll follow out this line of inquiry. Tell you what, I've got a hunch. You call in all the directors who were at that conference when Ireton was killed. We'll take 'em down to the morgue and let them have a look at the corpse. Maybe one of them can identify the man. If they can't, it'll be all to the good because there are one or two questions I want to ask those directors. I'm not satisfied about that gang yet."

By dint of much telephoning and argument with people who insisted they were busy, notably Mrs. Flood and Joseph McMurray, we finally contrived to get the people who had been present at the famous conference grouped in the office of the morgue. Beside La Flood and McMurray, there was Bennington Graeme, bound tightly with adhesive tape under his shirt. He grimaced with pain every time he moved without thinking; Harry Gruening, Van Gelder, Miss Curtain, Captain Treadfast. We had debated whether or not to call Larry Parsons, and had decided it would look as if we were bringing together the suspects rather than directors, if we called him. For that reason also Danny Mulroy, the publicity man, was not called.

I missed most of the fun because Tonelli chose to stand at the head of the slab upon which the body awaiting identification lay. He asked his questions over the bloated face. That guy could think of more ways of making a third degree disagreeable than any copper I ever knew.

I stood in the corridor outside the vault and watched them as they went in and came out. La Flood went in looking anxious and annoyed, and came out weeping and worried. McMurray, the musician, was pale gray when he went in, and a greenish-yellow when he came out. If he had any emotion other than retching of the diaphragm, I failed to see it. Bennington Graeme went in with a merry quip, and came out swearing softly under his breath. Harry Gruening, when the door opened for him, and he caught one glimpse of the sheeted form, squawked like a woman, then advanced steadily, answered his questions, and came out ablaze with excitement. He caught me by the coat lapel.

"That's amazing," he exclaimed. "Have you been in there? Have you seen that light? Have you seen the amazing composition that scene makes? That big slab in the middle of the floor, that sheeted body on it, that great brute Tonelli jutting up behind it like a mountain, that narrow compartment that held the body, that thing half drawer, half tomb? It's the first time I've ever been in a morgue. I know one of the boys on the project who could make a picture of it that would pull your heart right out of your body."

I calmed him down.

"It practically jerked my lunch out," I said. "I still have a heart."

Van Gelder went in and came out, with the bedside manner of a fashionable physician. Miss Curtain twittered and minced when she went in, and she minced and twittered when she came out. Treadfast, the doughty captain of engineers, went marching in with a face set and stern and came out with his handkerchief jammed hard against his mouth.

I said, "What's the matter, Captain? Can't you take it?"

His answer was more a gulp than a word, but *I* knew what he meant.

Tonelli told me he used exactly the same procedure with each visitor in turn. He had urged them to come closer to the body, and when they stood over it he turned down the sheet and let them look at the face. One by one they denied they'd ever seen the man, and Tonelli admitted he had noticed nothing that would tend to indicate any of them were lying. He then questioned them briefly about where they had been at the moment Commodore Ireton was killed, checking up on what they had told him right after the crime in the conference room. Allowing for the explainable and expected confusion, their stories held up well.

"So," Tonelli concluded, "we are exactly where we started, as far as this gang is concerned."

"Let's frame Izzie Jones and have it over with," I suggested.

Tonelli was too busy with sensible ideas to pay attention to me. He was a little weary as we once more took up the white man's burden. I got a taxi back to the office and, as instructed by Tonelli, had a search of the records begun which would give us the names of all people on WPA who had been absent from work on the day the corpse in the morgue had got its come-uppance. Tonelli at headquarters arranged to have the dead man photographed and distributed twenty-five prints among his plainclothesmen with instructions to circulate through the projects until they found somebody who would identify the man. He also sent an expert squad to the recreation park at the other side of the bridge to try to establish it as the scene of the killing. Then for the rest of the day I settled down to routine business in an endeavor to earn my salary from the United States, and deputy administrate something.

12

ALONG ABOUT A QUARTER TO FIVE, while I was in the midst of dictating a report, one hell of a row broke loose outside my office door. The bucktoothed stenographer dropped her book and shrank back in her chair, expecting every moment, I'm sure, to have a gang of murderers break in and kill us both. The row rose to crescendo, and the door burst open with Izzie Jones perspiring, pulling his coattails away from the messenger who had been posted out there to keep away Izzie's ilk of callers.

I said, "All right, his belly's in, that counts as a goal. Release his coattails and allow him to cover himself decently once more." Then to Izzie: "What in the name of the New Deal do you want now?"

"It's Mr. Parsons," Izzie gasped. "Mr. Lawrence Parsons. He's outside, he's got to see you."

I said to the buck-toothed stenographer, "Go on, get that stuff transcribed," and to Izzie, "What're you standing there for? Get him in here."

Larry's face was as long as the last mile from home. His coat was torn. His collar and tie were wrecked.

"What's happened to *you?*" I asked.

"Not me. Jaze," he gasped. "She's gone. Kidnapped."

"Oh my God," I groaned. "Why did you have to kidnap her? Couldn't you have eloped without the frills and thrills?"

"Not me," said Larry. "I didn't kidnap—"

Izzie took it upon himself to put everything straight.

"You don't understand," he explained to me. "Mr. Parsons says Miss Jaze Ireton is missing. She's gone."

"Why not tell it to the police?" I demanded. "I'm not the Bureau of Missing Persons."

"You can't trust the police," Izzie spoke dramatically. "This is a job we have to do ourselves. I've got a car downstairs waiting."

"Not me," I demurred. "You don't get me into another one of those cars. There're too many people around here handy with guns and brickbats."

I reached for the telephone.

"Get me Lieutenant Tonelli at headquarters, and make it snappy," I ordered.

"We're wasting time," Larry moaned. "She's gone, I tell you. She may have been gone for hours."

Tonelli came on the other end of the wire.

I said, "Pete, I'm sorry to disturb your peace and quiet again; but Larry Parsons is here in the office and says that Miss Ireton is missing. What do you know about it?"

"Miss Ireton," Pete told me, "left her home at nine o'clock this morning to visit her Aunt Margaret Ireton who lives in Bellaire. My men put her on the train, rode out there with her, and saw her safely into her aunt's house. She told them that she was going to stay there all afternoon, and they're going to pick her up again tonight at seven."

I covered the phone with my hand.

"Your sweetie's out at her aunt's in Bellaire," I said to Larry.

He shouted, "She isn't! I just came from there. I took the day off to be with her. Her aunt is not in town. We wanted to be alone. The house is empty, and I tell you there's nobody there!"

"Sound a general alarm," I said to Tonelli through the telephone. "Parsons says this was all a stall. He and the girl friend had it fixed up to have a quiet day alone in the country. The aunt isn't at home. The house is empty, and the gal is gone. Parsons just got back from there."

"Meet me at the L & M station in five minutes," Pete ordered. "And bring Parsons along with you."

"How did *you* get in on this?" I asked Izzie as I grabbed my hat and coat.

"I been trailing Mr. Parsons," Izzie admitted. "He's right, the girl isn't there."

As we were going down in the elevator, I asked Izzie: "Did you examine the house? Was there any sign of a struggle? Do you think the girl was kidnapped? Did you kidnap her?"

"I looked the house over," Izzie said. "It looked right to me. No, I didn't kidnap her," he added indignantly.

"What happened to *you?*" I asked Larry again. "How come you're all torn up and dirty?"

"I drove out," he said. "I've got an old car. While I was in the house something happened to the car. I was so worried and scared I got panicky. I did all this damage to myself trying to fix the damned thing."

I looked at Izzie.

"Honest," he said, "I wasn't trying to delay him just for meanness. I fixed the spark plugs when he went in the house because I didn't want him and the lady to make a getaway without me knowing it."

"You're a great help, Izzie," I commended him.

Tonelli came roaring up to the L & M station as we got there, although he had twice as far to ride. There was no train for three-quarters of an hour, but Tonelli checked with the ticket sellers and gate men, two of whom remembered seeing Jaze Ireton get on the morning train. They recognized her from her pictures in the paper.

We piled into Tonelli's car and split the breeze for Bellaire.

The house we reached after three-quarters of an hour's drive, was of colonial type, white clapboard, with eight or nine rooms, comfortable, and well-to-do but not opulent. The front door was locked. A pane of glass was shattered in the back door. Larry Parsons confessed he had been guilty of breaking it and entering when he had been unable to raise anybody by ringing the doorbell. He broke the glass in the back door, reached through and turned the key. Larry furnished the information that Miss Margaret Ireton lived there alone with a middle-aged woman to keep her company and act as housekeeper. They were off on a little cruise, Miss Ireton having been recommended a change of air by the doctor. She had offered to take Jaze with her, but Jaze had preferred to stay near Larry, although that was not the explanation she gave her aunt.

"Miss Margaret was all cut up over the Commodore's death," Larry explained. "You may remember her being at the Commodore's funeral."

"If she was the lantern-jawed battle-axe Jaze was with," I said, "I remember her well and unfavorably."

"That was her," said Larry.

Tonelli was at his eternal and intelligent snooping around. He ducked suddenly under the couch in the living room and pulled out a handkerchief. He smoothed it out and held it up for inspection.

"Do you recognize this?" he asked Larry.

"It looks like one of Jaze's," Larry said.

Tonelli put it in his pocket. He went over the whole house.

"Nothing here," he admitted at last. It seemed like a long time, but his inspection took rather less than ten minutes. He took down the telephone.

"Give me the chief operator," he said. "Hello, chief operator? This is Lieutenant Tonelli, headquarters. I want to trace, quickly as possible, all calls made to and from this house this morning. The number is Bellaire 0197, listed in the name of Miss Margaret Ireton."

While he was waiting for the information, he said to Larry:

"Why the hell didn't you telephone instead of coming all the way back to town? This trail is three or four hours old now."

Larry gulped.

"It's older than that," he admitted. "I was supposed to be here at ten o'clock this morning, but I had trouble with the car and I didn't get here until after eleven. When Jaze didn't answer the doorbell I thought she had got sore and gone back to town. I broke in the house just to make sure, and then I got scared. I called up her house, but there was no answer. I thought maybe she was peeved because I hadn't kept my date on time, and that she was having lunch somewhere in town. When my car didn't start I got kind of frantic, I guess, and I ran all the way to the station and went right to the Ireton house in town. Jaze wasn't there either, and so I went right up to the Administration Building."

"Why didn't you go to the police?" Tonelli asked him.

"You know how it is," Larry defended himself. "You don't like to think things are as bad as they look. I knew I was in a panic and thought maybe I was making some fool mistake. As I was leaving the Ireton house in town, Izzie Jones here came up to me. He asked me where Miss Ireton was, and I told him I didn't know, I was looking for her."

Izzie interrupted here.

"Then I said to him," said Izzie, "that he was crazy, that he was wasting a lot of time, that we had better get to the Administration Building as fast as possible. By then, I suspected Miss Ireton had been kidnapped."

I turned on Izzie.

"Then this kidnapping idea is all yours?" I said. "For all we know, Miss Ireton is somewhere downtown in a movie, watching Myrna Loy and Bill Powell carry on."

Tonelli at the telephone held up his hand for silence.

"What's that?" he asked again. "Repeat that, please. You say there were three calls, two outgoing and one incoming? One at ten-seventeen this morning to the station? What is that number?—Oh yes, the taxi company. And one into the city? About eleven-thirty?—Eleven thirty-two, you say?—Yes, that's Commodore Ireton's number. And what was the other call?—Was that a local call? Where was the call made from?—What is that, a drug store? Thank you very much. That's all, thanks."

He hung up.

"There was a call made here about ten o'clock this morning. I mean here in town. The call came from the pay station in the drug store down near the railroad. That call was answered in this house. Your girl called up to check on trains to the city at ten-seventeen. That must have been while she was getting mad at you, Parsons, for being late. The call that was made into Commodore Ireton's house was the one you made, Parsons. But that in-between incoming call was answered here in the house. Let's hop down to that drug store."

The proprietor of the drug store was also the prescription counter man and the soda clerk. He recalled that two men had driven up to the store, shortly before or after ten o'clock, but right around ten o'clock. That one of them had stayed outside in the car, which was a standard make, black sedan; the other one had bought a package of cigarettes and had made a phone call. Both men got into the car and drove off immediately after the phone call was made.

While Tonelli was questioning the drug store proprietor, two plainclothesmen I recognized as members of his squad, came up to him and stood waiting to report.

Tonelli finished with the proprietor, and one of the plainclothesmen spoke up:

"We checked the houses on both sides of Miss Margaret Ireton's house here in the village, and we talked to Mrs. Peters across the street. She certainly is full of scandal, Chief. She called young Miss Ireton a hussy. She said she had been coming out here meeting some man ever since her aunt left."

Tonelli cut in: "Did you get a description of the man?"

Larry said uncomfortably: "That's not necessary. I'm the man."

The plainclothesman resumed. "About ten-thirty the old busybody reports, two gents drove up in a black car. She couldn't tell whether the car was a Chevvy or a Nash or a Dodge, or what it was. She don't know nothing about cars. All she knows about is her neighbors' business. She's got the blinds in front of her house pulled down with one of them raised just about two inches from the sill. She sets there all day and peeps out, and makes up bedtime stories for herself."

"Never mind about her," Tonelli snapped. "Get on with what she told you."

"Well, she says Miss Ireton came out of the house with the two men. She couldn't see so good, because the car was in her way, but she's sure Miss Ireton walked out by herself and she was not bound or gagged or carried. The three of them got into the car and drove away."

"Which way did they drive?" Tonelli asked.

"To the north, toward the main interurban highway. Then along about eleven o'clock or after, the gent who's been coming out here came driving up in an old rattletrap car, and he got out and tried to get into the house."

"That was me," said Larry. "And Jaze and I came only once before. That was yesterday."

"That's all the old dame knew, and that's all we could get from any of the neighbors," the plainclothesman finished up his report.

"Okay," said Tonelli. "You drive over to the highway, get hold of one of the State Troopers of the Highway Patrol, and see if you can trace that black sedan."

The two plainclothesmen hurried out.

Tonelli said, "All right, let's go."

I said, "Go where?"

"Over to the real estate office, of course," said Tonelli. It was in the same block with the drug store across from the station.

The real estate agent was very glad to see us. He thought we were prospects for a new house. Tonelli made short work of that hope. He flashed his badge and said brusquely:

"Have you see anything today of two men who were looking for a house over Oak Lawn way?"

"Why yes," said the real estate agent. "They were very much interested in property over that way. They looked over the plans of several houses."

"Any one particular they thought they might like?" Tonelli inquired.

"They seemed most interested in Miss Ireton's house," said the agent. "They went over all the plans very carefully."

"Can you describe these men?" Tonelli demanded.

"I think so," the real estate man puzzled. "One of them was—oh, a man of thirty-five or forty years of age, smooth-shaven, square-faced, about medium height or a little taller; say five feet, eight. The other man was a little bit shorter, sallow complected, thin-faced, with a rather long nose. He was a very quiet man. The other man was more genial, and did a great deal more talking."

"What kind of car did they drive?" Tonelli asked.

"Why, a Monogram Six, a black sedan," the real estate man answered instantly.

"May I use your telephone?" Tonelli asked, and without awaiting permission, grabbed the instrument. "Give me State Police Headquarters, official," he barked. "Hello, this is Lieutenant Tonelli of headquarters. Put out the dragnet for a Monogram Six black sedan. It is driven by a man five feet, eight inches tall, square face, wearing a gray felt hat and a brown overcoat. He is accompanied by a smaller

man with a sallow complexion in a black overcoat and a gray hat.
There is a woman with them. About twenty-five years of age. Dark
brown hair, gray eyes, wearing a red hat, black coat with a mink fur
collar, and a black tailored dress. She had on black suede pumps,
and reddish brown stockings. This woman is Miss Jane Esmerelda
Ireton. Hold the two men if apprehended, as suspected kidnappers.
Get hopping. When last seen the black sedan was travelling north
from the suburb of Bellaire on the interurban highway. That was
between ten-thirty and eleven o'clock this morning."

"Fat lot of good that will do us," Tonelli commented as he disconnected, "but we've got to cover all the angles."

"And as for you," I turned on Izzie, "you're pretty much responsible for messing this thing up. What in hell are you following Mr.
Parsons for?"

"Well," Izzie shrugged his shoulders, "*somebody* murdered the
Commodore."

On the way back to town Tonelli told us about the dragnet he
had thrown out in the city. Every available detective and patrolman
was checking with all of Jaze's known friends and relatives, in the
hope of finding her, or of obtaining some clue to her whereabouts.
My guess that she was in a movie had also occurred to Tonelli, and
police were searching every movie house in the city. That would be
done without the movie patrons ever being aware of it. The film
would snap, and the lights in the house would go up. The manager
would come up to the stage or call from the back of the house and
ask the patrons to be patient, and the policeman would inspect every
row from the side and center aisles. While he was making his investigation, women ushers would take a look into the dressing rooms
and smoking lounge.

Through the teletype and radio cars the whole thing could
be done with extraordinary speed. All of the thousands of men at
the disposal of the police department would drop everything else
for this emergency. Within an hour or so Tonelli could be reasonably certain that Jaze was not with friends or relatives, not in the
theatres, and not in any hotel or restaurant or other public place.
The department stores were much more difficult to check, because

of the great volume of people constantly flowing in and out. Nevertheless even there policemen placed at each of the entrances and at bus stops at the principal points downtown would watch for her. He had set this machinery in motion before joining us at the station.

Larry Parsons was all for dashing about, poking his nose into places hither and yon, looking for his beloved; but I persuaded him there was nothing he could do, and to ease his jitters took him home with me. After he'd had a hot shower, some clean clothes, something to eat, and the hotel valet had mended his coat, he was less wild but no less worried. I ordered up a jug of Scotch, and we proceeded to wrap ourselves around it. For the plain meanness of it, I ordered Izzie to stand by but explained to him his face gave me a pain and therefore stationed him downstairs in one of the public parlors, with the evening newspapers. It seemed to me best to have him under my thumb for the moment. I had suggested to Tonelli that we let him go and have him followed in the hope he might lead us to something, but Tonelli hadn't the men to spare.

Tonelli, I found, had great respect for Izzie. Izzie was not the easiest man in the world to tail. Time and again he had eluded some of Tonelli's best operators, and there was much about his private life the police had been unable to ferret out.

So Izzie sat in the parlor, reading the scareheads on the disappearance of Miss Ireton, and Larry and I sat in my room and gargled liquor.

Around nine o'clock, Bennington Graeme dragged himself in to see me. He said his ribs felt like Sandow had used them for a xylophone; but the sticking plaster the docs had wound around him held him together. It was fun, he explained, when the adhesive tape had to be changed. He said his doctor had an office nurse who was a knockout, but she was a sadistic wench and stood laughing while his doc ripped off adhesive tape and hair and hide with it. I gathered as soon as Bennington could use his arms without stabbing pains in the region of his ribs, his doctor's office nurse was due for a complete workout. Mr. Graeme explained his strategy with the nurse in an endeavor to get Larry Parsons' mind off his own sweetie.

Benny said he was using the slow approach. He had taken the gal out to lunch, and been very careful of what he said and did. He then took her to the movies and to dinner, and gradually he was working up to the point so that when he got his health he would be ready to go to it and she would be disarmed by his innocence and gentlemanly candor.

In the midst of this tale of conjectural amours, Benny shuddered and set down his glass.

"Damn it all," he said, "I can't get the thought of that drowned man's face out of my mind."

I poured him another drink, a good stiff one, and he took it at a gulp. It revived him sufficiently to launch him forth on some more details of his strategy with the nurse. It seemed the young lady was somewhat enamored of an interne at the City Hospital. She was worried about the goings on between the hospital staff and the probationers. And well she might worry, said Benny, recalling his own sojourn in the hospital. While he had been there, the young ladies who worked on his floor assumed he was a good egg, and his room became a meeting place where doctors and nurses exchanged greetings, usually behind the screen in the corner.

I said, "Oh, Benny!"

"Not what you think," he said, "you dirty low-minded hound."

"I don't know how you guys can sit around and talk like this," Larry lamented. "Haven't you got any hearts? For all we know, Jaze may be dead while we're sitting here."

Benny struck his forehead with his open palm, "'Dead,'" he said, "that word makes me think of Mister Bloated Face again. I know I've seen that guy somewhere."

"Probably in some bar," I comforted him.

Benny set his glass down with a thump.

"That's it!" he said. "I remember now. I *have* seen that face in a bar."

He grew thoughtful, sank back in his chair, picked up his glass and filled it absent-mindedly.

"Let me think," he murmured. "Did I see him in a bar? There's something about him I've got connected in my mind with a bar."

I said facetiously, "Crossing the bar? Moaning at the bar? Prisoner at the bar? If—"

Benny snapped his fingers.

"That does it," he exclaimed. "Prisoner at the bar. The guy's a lawyer!"

I was interested now. I said, "Where?"

"Why damn it," said Benny, "he's on my own project; it was the bloated face that fooled me. The guy isn't half bad looking when he's alive."

I said, "Yes, this light-minded dying hither and yon does spoil one's features. Now tell me, *where* on your project, *what* on your project, *how* on your project, is, or was, this guy a lawyer, and what is his name, and what does he do?"

Benny waved me away with an ineffectual hand.

"I asked for him," he said, "couple of weeks ago. I need a lawyer on the project. You see, we're doing a city guide, and we have to do considerable research work. We need some baby who can translate legal verbiage and technical terms of the law. So, we have to have a lawyer. We've got anything you want on the Writers' Project. From A to Z. From an Anthropologist to a Zoologist."

"Let's stick around with the L's," I suggested. "You say you asked for this fellow a couple of weeks ago?"

"Well, it might have been a couple of months ago. Anyway, it hasn't been long now. Reason I didn't remember the fellow right away is because I've only seen him once. I asked for him the other day, and they told me he was away. He certainly was. 'Way, far away, floating in the river."

Here, Benny began to sing, "I Was Floating Down the Old Green River, on the Good Ship Rock and Rye. I must have floated too far—"

Larry, who had drunk quite as much as Benny, but whose troubles made the liquor so much water, was disgusted. He got up and went into the bathroom, closing the door with a bang.

I caught Benny's shoulder and he winced. I said to him: "Listen, Benny—this is very serious. Think. Think hard. Get sober, quick. This may be an important clue for Tonelli. Tell me all you know about this lawyer. Do you know his name?"

Benny blinked. "No," he said. "Don't be so rough. Every time you grab me like that and shake me I can feel the ends of my ribs grind together. If I didn't have all this liquor in me, I'd be screaming with the pain."

"If you don't snap out of it," I threatened, "I'll kick in your ribs, what's left of them. Now," I went to the phone and ordered black coffee, "drink this when it gets here, and get lucid quickly. I want to know all about this lawyer on the Writers' Project as fast as God will let you think."

I might just as well have phoned Tonelli then. I could get nothing more out of Graeme. He had needed a lawyer, he had asked Personnel for a lawyer, he had got a lawyer. He didn't know when the man came to work, how long he had worked, and he didn't know how long the man had been absent from the job. Looked like we would have to wait until morning to get the record.

Headquarters gave me one of the sergeants on Tonelli's squad, instead of the Lieutenant who was out on some phase of the case. I dictated the meagre information I had been able to wring out of Bennington Graeme, and sat down to think it all over.

Larry paced the floor like a caged tiger, Bennington leaned stiffly back in his chair and absorbed my Scotch. It was a jolly evening.

Came a ring on the telephone, Tonelli calling.

"Say," he said, "I called up the office and they told me about your message. Is that the correct dope about this stiff we've got in the morgue?"

"Correct as far as I've got it," I said. "We don't know his name, we don't know where he came from, we don't know where he lives or how long he worked, but Bennington Graeme is sure he is the lawyer he requisitioned through the Personnel office."

"Where do they get lawyers from in the WPA?" Tonelli demanded. "Has the WPA got a legal project?"

That was something to think of.

"I never heard of a legal project," I confessed. "But there are a lot of lawyers around. We use lawyers for a lot of things. They're very necessary at times."

I could hear the grin in Tonelli's voice as he answered:

"That's what a lot of my friends among the crooks tell me. There's nothing like a good lawyer when you're in a jam."

Bennington Graeme looked up blandly to say: "Do you want to know what project has got a lot of lawyers on it?"

I said into the transmitter, "Wait a minute, Tonelli." And then to Graeme, "Yes, Mr. Broken Bones, what project has a lot of lawyers?"

He said, "Why Mr. Tambo, the Research Project has a lot of lawyers. They ain't got nothing else but. Boy lawyers and girl lawyers. They spend all their time digging into musty records, down at the courthouse, and tabulating and filing them correctly. I don't know why, you don't know why, Van Gelder don't know why, there's no explanation except that it's the WPA."

To Tonelli I said, "Sorry, Pete. Nothing more. My news source is as boiled as a dress shirt. What comforting words have you got I can relay to my friend Larry Parsons?"

"That's a tough one," said Pete mournfully. "I haven't got a line for the kid. We haven't picked up anything. No clues, nobody's seen her, there are millions of black sedans, and all of them've got two men and a girl in 'em. I dunno what you can tell the kid. Just tell him to sit tight."

Cheerily I chirped as I hung up: "Lieutenant Tonelli says to tell you that everything looks fine, Larry. He says he oughta have a report for you in the next hour or so. Anyway, before morning. Everything's under control. They've got a red-hot clue, and it doesn't look like a kidnapping at all."

Larry's voice was haggard.

"That's a swell line, Jim," he said. "I know it's all a pack of lies. Tonelli's men haven't been able to find out a goddam thing, have they?"

I poured him a drink and handed it to him silently.

He gulped it, drew back his arm and crashed the tumbler into the plate glass mirror on the bureau. It made a very satisfactory crash, and it relieved my feelings almost as much as his.

Benny, who had been dozing, sat up and asked: "Thunder?"

I said to Larry:

"You're right, kid. Come on, let's go. Anything's better than sitting around here waiting for the telephone to ring."

Together we went downstairs, and in the lobby I remembered Izzie.

I found him sound asleep in a Louis Quinze chair which set off his beauty admirably.

I shook him awake.

"Come on, dope," I said. "Mr. Parsons and I are going out places to look for Miss Ireton. Come along and help."

He stumbled to his feet.

"I've got an idea," he admitted. "Do you want to follow it up?"

"Sure," I said. "If you've got an idea, that's one more than I've got. Lead us to it."

"It may lead to a lot of trouble," Izzie hedged.

"That's just dandy," I told him. "I haven't had any trouble since I've been here. A little good old-fashioned trouble would put me on my feet."

I stopped by the desk and left word with the night clerk that if anybody called me to say I'd be back in an hour; and that in case Lieutenant Tonelli called, he was to be informed that I had gone out in an official car with Mr. Izzie Jones and Mr. Lawrence Parsons.

As I turned away from the desk, I saw the door leading to the stairway at the side of the elevator shaft open and Bennington Graeme slipped out.

He was as sober as a judge.

13

PERSONALLY, I COULD HAVE DONE with a great deal less scenery. By the time we had cleared the city limits and were heading along into the open country, what common sense I had was beginning to reassert itself and I was regretting, in a small way, I had allowed myself again to be inveigled into the clutches of Izzie Jones.

Larry Parsons was in the condition when a man walks in front of rapidly approaching railway trains and steps into open manholes. He would have gone anywhere, and done anything that was suggested, as long as he kept moving and active.

While Izzie attempted to make conversation, I tried to get a good look at the driver of the car. Not only had I let myself fall back on Izzie's tender mercies, but here I was in another one of those big official hearses I had sworn never to use again. The driver kept his eyes rigidly front, which was just as well considering the speed we were making; but to my heightened suspicions, this circumstance was ominous.

"Izzie," I said, "you know this driver well, don't you?"

"Yes indeed," Izzie assured me. "He is a perfectly trustworthy man. He's a potty member."

"Potty?" I muttered. "Potty—he's far less potty than I. *He's* getting paid by the mile for making this trip."

Izzie explained. He whispered hoarsely:

"*The* Potty. You know. The Communist Potty. I thought you would like that."

"Oho!" said I. "A Red, eh? Where's his whiskers?"

Izzie said very seriously:

"He wouldn't need whiskers. None of us would need disguises tonight."

I said, "Izzie, have I ever seen that driver before?"

"You could look for yourself," Izzie suggested.

"There is something about the back of that guy's head that reminds me of broken windows and cobblestones and shots in the dark," I said.

Larry came out of his stupor long enough to remark, "That's a hell of a lot to be reminded of by the back of a man's head."

We were passing through a district given over to factory buildings, and passing through with a great deal of celerity. Beyond the clump of sordid houses and frowning, smoke-stained buildings we came again to open road. Farmhouses began to show up. Small places at first, an acre or half acre at the most; then a village, a few more straggling houses, and a clear stretch of road for half a mile or more with no buildings at all. From then on the buildings were at widely-spaced intervals.

"Nice country you have around here," I said to Izzie. "Don't you think it's about time you explained the purpose of this moonlight drive? Or are you taking us to join Jaze Ireton?"

"If I have guessed right," said Izzie, "that is exactly where I am taking you."

"What do you mean, guessed?" said I. "You seem to know pretty well where you're going. And if you don't, you ought to."

Izzie shrugged expressively.

"What do you do in the WPA anyhow, Izzie?" I asked him.

Izzie wriggled in his seat.

"I'm supposed to be head of the Radio Project," Izzie confessed, "but there is some trouble about it. Nobody seems to want to give it any people or money."

Uncharitably I said: "Well, if what it takes to run radio is a lousy, double-crossing, unreliable child of mixed and undesirable parentage, you are perfectly fitted to the job, Izzie, my friend."

His thick lips caressed the dead and smelly stump of a cigar and he looked unhappy but not spirited enough to resent an insult.

He also looked very uncomfortable with his bulk overflowing one of the folding chairs. There was room for him on the back seat where

Larry and I sat, but Izzie had declined the honor of squeezing in between us. I knew he must be sawed in two by the saddle he was straddling, but he made no complaint and was as moon-facedly unctuous as ever. A more genial and humble ruffian than Izzie never slit a throat.

We turned off the paved highway into a black macadam road which wound along between rows of trees, fences, and hedges. Once we passed the gate of a private estate or country club. The headlights of our car would shoot out at high trajectory as we nipped up the little rises; and then there would be a yawning cavern under our front wheels until the lights again dropped onto the road as we topped the crests.

Our pace was slowed by the twisting road which got rougher as we progressed further into the back country. Farmhouses became scarce indeed. For ten minutes we rode without seeing so much as a barn.

Izzie leaned forward and tapped the driver on the shoulder.

"Go easy from now on," he said. "I'll tell you where to turn."

We bumped along at a hand pace, with Izzie watching intently ahead for some landmark known only to him. Our lights picked out a clump of mailboxes by the side of the road, and Izzie again spoke to the driver.

"The side road is just a few feet beyond those mailboxes. You'll have to turn sharp right and go slowly, because that's just a dirt road."

It had been dry for some days and this new road was deeply rutted and eroded. Loose pebbles shot out from under our wheels and banged up against the mudguards. We were climbing steadily, not a steep grade but a gradual one, that continually mounted. Izzie spoke again anxiously to the driver.

"Watch sharp," he cautioned. "If you see anything like the headlights of a car coming down this way, drive into the bushes at the side of the road, and get out of sight if possible." To us he said, "It won't be long now."

None of us saw any lights, and after some fifteen more minutes of creeping, Izzie gave the word. There was an open clearing just off the track, and we turned into that, rolling along the firm turf until the car was well hidden from passersby in a dense growth of scrub oak fringed by tall sumac bushes.

"We walk from here on," said Izzie. He produced two flashlights, and asked me, "Have you got a gun?"

"Yes," I lied. I was not going to let Izzie know he had us at his mercy. Larry said he was unarmed.

The driver squirmed but Izzie relieved him by ordering him to switch off his lights and to stand by the car. Then Izzie led the way straight into the heart of the scrub oak grove.

Occasionally he would flash his light to indicate a rock or a fallen branch. Our eyes became accustomed to the darkness, and we could see the faint thread of a path. Still we were climbing, still that gentle ever ascending upgrade and a sense of being miles away from any human contact.

The sweat began running down my back. My long overcoat impeded my progress and I opened it both for air and for greater freedom of motion. Behind me I could hear Larry stumbling and cursing now and then. If his thin city shoes tortured his feet as much as mine did, I couldn't blame him. We did not talk. When we spoke we spoke in whispers. Izzie had said nothing about quiet, but set an example which we followed.

Fifteen or twenty minutes we slogged along up, always climbing, and eventually came out of the trees. Izzie paused to let Larry and me come up abreast of him. We were on the flat top of a hill, and could see a considerable distance in all directions, even in the dark. Below us, just under the crest of the hill, lay a clump of farm buildings with a road curving around from the hillside to pass the door of the dwelling. It was the continuation of the road we had come along in the car. There were no lights in the house. The place was asleep, or deserted as far as we could tell.

Izzie put his lips close to my ear.

"The girl," he said, "is down there in that house, I think."

"Whose house is it?" I asked.

"It belongs to a farmer in the neighborhood, but it is rented to city people. The farmers around here call it the Club. The men who rent the place have let it be understood that they come up here to hunt and fish and maybe get away from their wives for week-ends. The farmers think they have liquor and gambling sessions here."

"Still," I whispered angrily, "you haven't told me who is really in the house. Is it your house?"

"It is not mine," Izzie said. "I think it is the headquarters of the Confidence Corps of the Four-Square Americans."

"Do you expect to walk into that hornet's nest?" I asked. "Unarmed? Just the three of us?"

"Oh no," Izzie was indignant at my criticism of his tactics. "We'll only look around and see if we can find any evidence to pass on to the police."

"Come on, we can't expect to live forever," Larry growled.

We went quietly downhill, each choosing his own path. Every broken twig sounded like a cannon shot. It took us two extremely long and scary minutes to scramble down into the shadow of the barn. Once there, the three of us crouched in the deep shadow and held a conference.

Izzie made disposition of forces.

"Mr. Moore," he said, "you and Mr. Parsons take the right hand side. You go out around the barn and circle the house. Keep in the shadows so nobody can see you, and try and find out if there's anybody inside. I'll go in the other direction and we'll meet on the far side of the house."

I motioned to Larry, and we crept around the end of the barn and the outside of the barnyard. There were no trees shielding the house. The space between the barn and the house was bare. No flowers, no grass to speak of. It had sounded very prudent and considerate for Izzie to talk about keeping in the shadows, but there were no shadows in which to keep.

I whispered to Larry: "I feel like I was standing out against the skyline like the top twenty stories of the Empire State building."

"So do I," he said, "only I'm the Washington Monument."

We got safely across the interval between the barn and the house, halted under one of the lower windows and attempted to peer in. The blind was drawn. There was no sound, from within, no light. Stealthily we continued our circuit. Under the high front porch, out to the far side of the house. There were two windows on this side, and we crawled along under them to look but they were shuttered. I crept on as planned, saw Izzie coming from his end of the patrol, and walked forward to meet him.

I whispered, "What luck, Izzie?" and the man confronting me answered by shoving an automatic against my belt buckle and ordering:

"Stick 'em up."

I raised my hands shoulder high, and backed away from him. Behind me there was a scuffle, a gruff command. I heard Larry cry out, and metal thumped against something hard.

I looked back. Larry was on the ground, with two men bending over him, one with revolver raised to strike again if need be.

I said between my clenched teeth, "Izzie, you double-crossing son of a bitch, if I ever get out of this I'm going to kick that fat belly right off you."

The man holding the gun on me said, "Don't get excited, pal. Save your breath and stay healthy."

The two men who had smacked Larry down came past us, one on each side of Larry, dragging him by his arm pits. My friend motioned with the barrel of his gun and said, "Get around back. Follow them."

I started to pass between him and the house, which would have put me within striking distance of him, but he halted me.

"Keep your distance, buddy," he said. "I'm not takin' any chances on you jumping me. Walk around the outside, and get those hands up higher."

I backed around, facing him, and again he made that imperative motion with the pistol point saying:

"That's all right. You can turn your back on me. I kinda like the looks of your back. You don't need to follow no book of etiquette rules around here except what is suggested to you."

I preceded him around to the rear of the house. The back door was open. A kerosene lamp swung from the center of the kitchen, gave out a glare of light that was blinding to my eyes now used to the darkness. The man who had stopped me was a canny fellow. He didn't risk following me closely into the kitchen, where he would be equally blind. He stood below the back steps and watched me enter with my body making a beautiful silhouetted target against the lighted oblong of the door.

Inside there was a reception committee. They had let Larry slump to the floor, and his two captors stood with their pistols in their hands. Another man with drawn pistol stood right inside the door. Two men sat on a kitchen table, swinging their feet, a third was putting some coal on the cooking range which gave out a satisfying heat. There was no sign of Izzie anywhere.

The man who had escorted me in stumped up the steps and stood at the top, calling into the darkness by the barn:

"Is that all there are, Ed?"

From outside Ed answered:

"That's all there are. Three of 'em."

"All right," the first man called back. "You stay on watch and we'll relieve you in an hour. Keep your eye peeled for the other boys, and don't let anybody, friend or enemy, get near without giving us a signal."

He stepped inside, a big burly man with a black slouch hat and a sheepskin-lined short jacket. He glanced at me, then at Larry on the floor.

"Get that man up off the floor," he ordered. "And take the two of 'em"—the wave of his gun hand included me, "into the dining room."

One of the men lifted Larry to his feet, the other motioned me to precede him. I got service. The door leading into the interior of the house was close beside the kitchen table, and one of the men sitting on the table reached over, turned the knob, and swung the door inward. I marched through, saying over my shoulder:

"You boys certainly think of everything. I never saw a gang so anxious to keep away from a helpless man."

"Brother," said one of the men on the table, the same one who had opened the door, "you're about as helpless as a gorilla. I seen you in operation, down by the police station last night."

I said, "You've got me mixed up with my friend Tonelli. He's the fighter. I'm just a peaceful newspaperman trying to get along."

From the tail of my eye I caught a glimpse of him rubbing his cheek and grinning. He said,

"You'll get along all right." The man who had stuck me up spoke gruffly from the center of the floor:

"Hey, can the chatter. Whaddya think this is, a church sociable?"

The dining room was replete with a golden oak suite, chairs, table, china closet and sideboard, a red grosgrain carpet, and red and white checkered tablecloth. There was a steel engraving above the mantelpiece, entitled The Parting of the Lovers, in which a lad in a Hieland bonnet bade fond farewell to a lassie in a Juliet cap, while a horse who looked like he had escaped from a merry-go-round ogled impatiently over the garden wall. I shall draw that picture from memory someday. It impressed me, made the whole business more macabre.

Larry, dragged in behind me, was dumped into a rocking chair between the sideboard and the window, while I was allowed to sit down in a straight chair against the far wall. Two guards allotted to us lounged comfortably, one in each doorway. From the room in the front, which I took to be the parlor, came a murmur of voices, and I could gradually distinguish Izzie's frenzied accents.

"But Chief," I heard him say, "you know I'm a loyal member of the Order. I'm Four-Square, Chief."

Another voice murmured something I couldn't distinguish, and again Izzie's voice uprose.

"But I brought 'em straight here, didn't I?"

Words then ceased to be articulate and blended into a blur of sound in which I could hear Izzie's voice, then another's. Eventually came receding footsteps, two pairs, and the closing of a door. The door leading into the parlor jerked open, and another guard, sporting a pistol in a holster, beckoned to me.

"Come on in here," he ordered.

My feet ached abominably as I stood up, and I hobbled into a parlor that matched the dining room.

Pleasant, dry, pedantic tones greeted me.

"Well, Mr. Moore. I never expected to see *you* here."

It was my old friend, Van Gelder.

Dangling his pince-nez by its ribbon, he sat behind a scalloped marble-topped walnut table on which were spread some papers. All of the furniture in the room was of walnut, two decades preceding the golden oak period of the dining room. The sofa and chairs were upholstered in black haircloth. In addition, there was a whatnot complete with china ornaments and shells in one corner, a mantel shelf with more knickknacks, a "patented" rocking chair, and twin commodes with dangling black enamel and brass drawer-pulls.

I sat down in the rocker, facing Matthew Van Gelder. I thought of it as a gesture of defiance so I daresay I rather flounced.

"That's right," he said, "make yourself comfortable while you may."

"I don't like your tone, Mr. Van Gelder," I objected. "You sound as though I was not going to stay comfortable for long."

"That, to some extent, depends upon you," he assured me.

I looked around. "Where is Miss Ireton?" I asked.

"She is safe and sound, asleep by this time, I should judge," said Van Gelder affably.

"I trust she is quite comfortable," I ventured.

"Why shouldn't she be, in her father's cousin's house?" asked Van Gelder raising his eyebrows.

"Oh," I said dumbly, "does Commodore Ireton's cousin own this house?"

He smiled a tight smile.

"No," he said, "but he rents it. Didn't you know that *I* am Commodore Ireton's cousin?"

I gaped at him. I could hear Sarah Hirzner's gasping breath as she was dying, saying,

"Cursing—The Commodore's cussin'—"

"Good Lord!" I blurted out. "That's what she was trying to say. Not 'cussin',' but 'cousin.'"

"I do not know to whom you refer," Van Gelder said suavely, "but it sounds as though it might have some interest for me. Would you care to tell me more about it? Does it affect me?"

"It may have the effect of hanging you," I threatened.

He smiled his tight smile again.

"I hardly think so," he murmured. "I have been very careful in eliminating witnesses and evidence. I do not think I will hang, yet awhile."

"You know, of course," I bluffed, "that we left a car behind us when we walked up through the woods. The chauffeur had instructions to go back to town for help. The police are on their way here now."

"You are very naïve, and something of an optimist, friend Moore," he told me. "Listen."

I could hear voices and trampling feet in the dining room. A man stuck his head in, and reported:

"We got the chauffeur, Chief. We got him in here, anytime you're ready for him."

"He is not really important," Van Gelder told his man. "Just see that he doesn't create any disturbance, and we will get around to him when the time comes. In the meanwhile, give orders that I am not to be disturbed. Mr. Moore and I have a great many things in common to discuss. We have many mutual friends."

"I'm looking forward to this chat with the utmost eagerness," I said as blandly as I might.

14

"Mr. Moore," said Van Gelder, "how much money do you make?"

"Not enough," I said.

"Certainly not," he agreed affably. "I can understand that. But just between us here, and to go no further, what is your salary?"

"When I came up here," I told him, "I was put on the payroll as an expert. My pay is $25 per day, not to exceed four days' salary in any one week."

"In other words," said Van Gelder, "your salary is $5200 a year."

"Yes," I agreed, "unless, of course, I rate a rise in view of my new position as Acting Deputy Administrator."

"At the best," Van Gelder spoke judicially, "I doubt that you will receive more than six or seven thousand dollars. And that is far too little, for a man of your talents. I could use you, Mr. Moore. I could put you in the way of making considerable sums of money."

"In return for what?" I asked.

"Very little," he assured me. "Primarily, that you allow me to return you quietly to your hotel, and that you forget all about tonight's expedition."

I pretended to think this over. "What about Izzie Jones and Larry?" I asked.

"They'll be taken care of," Van Gelder assured me. "You may have guessed by now that Jones is one of us."

"I imagined as much," I told him.

"Does the proposition sound attractive to you?" he asked me.

I never had a chance to answer that question.

The door opened behind me, and someone stomped into the room; a heavy hand fell on my shoulder. I jumped up and found myself looking into the eyes of the guard from whom I had taken the pistol during the WPA riot on the day of my arrival. 'There was a nasty look in his eye as he greeted me.

"Hello, rat."

I said, "Well, well, well. Journeys end in lovers' meetings."

The man was completely deficient in a sense of humor. His lip curled, and his canines showed. He began that habitual gesture of his toward his hip pocket, but Van Gelder's voice, dry and emotionless, broke in.

"None of that," he ordered. "There's ample time for that sort of thing. Mr. Moore is considering joining us."

"Not him," the guard said. "He's a rat. Once a rat, always a rat. He'll sell us out. Better let me polish him off."

"I'm quite sure," Van Gelder maintained his dry tone, "that if Mr. Moore gives us his word, he will keep it. Indeed, I have reason to believe that we will be able to make him keep his word."

My pistol-toting friend backed a step away from me, completely unconvinced.

I said to Van Gelder, "What about Jaze Ireton? No matter what I promise, it might be difficult to explain where she has been, and if you let her go she will talk."

"I think not," said Van Gelder positively. He waved his hand in dismissal to the pug who still glowered at me.

"Okay, Chief," that worthy growled. "But you're takin' an awful chance."

"I think not," said Van Gelder again.

I took my seat in the rocker once more as the man left us. Van Gelder and I sat and looked at each other.

"Your entrance into this matter presents some difficulties," Van Gelder said with the air of a man who wanted to talk things over reasonably, and come to some compromise agreeable to both parties. "It is evident that you were sent up here from Washington on a special mission. Would you be divulging confidences to tell me exactly what your mission here is?"

"I'm quite sure it's no state secret," I assured him. "They were uneasy in Washington about this district, and they sent me up here to make a survey and a report. I had no definite instructions beyond that, until after Commodore Ireton's death, when I was authorized to take over the administration of the district temporarily."

"You are an ambitious young man," Van Gelder stated.

I nodded my head.

"Very probably it has already occurred to you that the position of WPA Administrator could be a stepping stone to much bigger things politically," he continued.

I nodded again.

"That being the case, it would be a great feather in your cap, Mr. Moore, if you were to be confirmed as Administrator of this district, and it would be an even greater credit to you if under your administration all signs of disorder and rebellion were to disappear."

I laughed. "That seems hardly possible."

"It is not only possible, but probable," Van Gelder said seriously. "We have a great deal of power, Mr. Moore, in this city and in this state. It could be arranged for you to be confirmed as Administrator. I could guarantee you personally that the entire strength of an organization I will not name now will be placed at your disposal to keep all WPA workers in this city and in your district well in hand."

"That organization wouldn't by any chance be the Four-Square Americans?" I inquired.

"I'm glad to see that I have not underestimated you, Mr. Moore," Van Gelder said suavely. "The Four-Square Americans are headed in the direction of tremendous power. I can assure you that not only will you be confirmed as Administrator, if you will throw in your lot with us, but we will advance you along the line. To Congress. To the Governorship. To the United States Senate, possibly even to the Presidency."

"That's a pretty attractive proposition," I said. "What would I have to do in return?"

"Nothing that should offend the dictates of your conscience, Mr. Moore. If you know anything of the Four-Square Americans, you know that the tenets of our creed are the fundamentals of civic and moral decency. No man can go far wrong who builds on a foundation of country, church, and the family. This organization—"

The effectiveness of what promised to be a well-rounded period was spoiled by a sound of a woman's voice. A shriek, rising and rising in jagged crescendo. It was Jaze Ireton's voice. I could recognize it, even in that desperate cry for help.

The sound pulled me to my feet and took me a step toward the door. The dry tones of the man at the table stopped me.

"I shouldn't pay too much attention to stray sounds, Mr. Moore," Van Gelder said. "Young women when they are kept from doing exactly what they like are apt to get hysterical. Don't allow yourself to get the same way."

I whirled in my tracks and found Van Gelder had me covered with an automatic in a hand rested and braced comfortably and firmly on the table top.

I said, "Oh," and with that eloquent speech returned to my chair and sat down. There was no further sound from Jaze.

"You see, Mr. Van Gelder," I said, "I am still a little jumpy. To one who knows exactly what is going on, the events of the past few days may look rather routine. But to an outsider such as I, the whole thing seems involved and mysterious."

"What things are particularly mysterious, Mr. Moore?"

"There was Commodore Ireton's death, to begin with," I said.

Van Gelder smiled.

"Unpleasant, but hardly mysterious," he contradicted me. "Somebody choked him to death. There is no mystery about that. He had many enemies."

"Then," said I, "there was the death of Sarah Hirzner."

"Mere coincidence," Van Gelder shrugged that off. "The young woman had been interested in her relationships with Commodore Ireton, and some young man who resented her—shall we say—misplaced affections, eliminated her."

"And then," I said, "there was the man whose body was found in the river, and whose identification card indicated he was John O. Martin."

Van Gelder raised his eyebrows. "Have you reason to believe that such was not his name?" he asked.

"I know there is another John O. Martin on WPA payroll," I said.

"This man you say they found in the river; was *he* a WPA employee?" asked Van Gelder. "And if so, what possible connection could his death have with the others?"

As affably as I could, I said, "Well, Mr. Van Gelder, when you put it like that, it certainly does seem that I have succumbed to a bad attack of the jitters over a series of coincidences."

Van Gelder was thoughtful. "Should you decide, Mr. Moore, to cast your lot in with ours, I would suggest to you that in the future you worry a little less about such obviously non-official things as these we have been discussing. You will have ample to do in maintaining your own position within the boundaries of your own authority."

I agreed that was correct.

He said, "I'm not going to rush you into an immediate decision. I'm going to give you a little time to think the matter over. I'm going to bring in your friend, Mr. Parsons, and have a little chat with him. In the meantime you can go back with the boys in the dining room and make up your mind."

He rapped sharply with the butt end of his pencil on the marble topped table, and both doors opened simultaneously, with a guard in each. He said to the man from the dining room, "Take Mr. Moore in and make him comfortable. Bring Mr. Parsons in here, and stand by for orders."

I tried to throw Larry a reassuring smile as we passed, but I don't believe he saw me. The gorilla who had broken into my interview with Van Gelder was waiting in the dining room. I sat down in the rocking chair in which Larry had sprawled, and thought over events. One of the other guards said to my particular friend:

"So this is the guy that took your gun away from you, huh? He don't look so big and strong to me, George."

George glowered. "He couldn'ta done it if he hadn't jumped me from behind," he said.

I spoke up sweetly, "Oh yes, I could," I boasted. "I can take a gun away from you anytime. In the first place, I'm a better man than you are; and for another thing, I'm quicker than you are; and, for the final thing, *you* haven't got the guts to shoot anybody who looked you in the eye."

The guard who had started to bait George, a rangy sandy-haired man, said: "That's telling you, George."

George said, "Aah, it's easy enough for him to talk, he knows the Chief wants to keep him on ice for a while."

"That's news to me," I said. "Hasn't told me anything about that. I'm a prisoner here. If you're such a big guy and such a tough mug, you could start in on me now. The reason you don't is that you're yellow. If all your pals here jumped in to help you, you might try to beat me up, but you wouldn't tackle it alone."

Sandy guffawed. "George," he said, "that boy packs a powerful line of chatter. Why'ntcha take one crack at him, for luck?"

I said, "Yeah, George, why don't you?"

George jumped up. He shed his heavy outside coat and the cardigan jacket under it, and rushed over to where I sat.

I said, "What are the rules around here? Can I move out of this chair without being filled with lead?"

The other three men came closer, forming a little ring around George, who stood over me.

Sandy spoke up. "I won't plug ya," he said.

Relying upon this sportsman having voiced the sentiment of the rest, I came out of the chair as fast as my legs would lift me. George, totally unprepared, got the top of my head in his face as I came upright. To make matters more hectic for him, I let go a one-two in his midriff; and when he doubled over, let him have it in the chin with my knee. It was all too much for George, who had probably learned his fighting in a more gentlemanly school. He was out cold. I straightened up, looked at my three regular guards and laughed.

"Well," I said, "there's George. And he never made a move for his gun."

I leaned over casually and rolled George over on his face as though it were all part of the demonstration, deliberately fumbled in his hip pocket, and pulled out his gun. When I straightened up I had my three boy friends covered.

"By gawd," said one of the guards, "he said he was gonna beat George up and take his gun away from him, and so he has!"

Sandy, who had been caught as flatfooted as the rest by the ingenuousness of my stunt, was not as naïve as his friend. He said, "Yeah, and now he's got us covered. Did you notice that?"

From the kitchen doorway a voice drawled, "I been noticin' right smart. But *I* got *him* covered. 's too bad, kid; you oughta got away with it."

I turned my head. In the doorway stood the man who had captured me outside the house. Sandy had the gun out of my hand on the instant.

They dragged George out into the kitchen, where I heard water splash and presently George began to curse. Then the outside door banged, and I heard no more of George. Meanwhile Sandy kept me covered from a safe and sane distance.

He jerked his head in the direction of the parlor and asked: "Did the Old Man give you a chance to join up?"

"Yes," I admitted.

"Better think it over," he advised. He jerked his head again in the general direction of the parlor. "The Old Man has read a lotta books, all about them old-time tortures. He's got one jim-dandy. He had the boys roll a big hogshead down the cellar and fill it fulla water. He takes people he don't like and takes off all their clothes, and just puts 'em in the hogshead. The cover has got round holes sawed in it, just big enough to fit around your neck, and he locks that down so you stay there till he's ready for you to come out. Don't sound very bad, if you say it fast, but it gets awful tiresome standin' up to your neck in water for three-four days at a time. Lotsa fellows have changed their minds in that hogshead."

I said that I didn't need a bath, and that as a matter of fact I was thinking over joining the organization.

"It's a pretty good outfit," Sandy assured me.

The two guards who had dragged George out came clumping back, and one of them slapped me playfully on the back of the head as he passed.

"I dunno anything about you, kid," he said, "but you certainly made a fool outa George."

Larry Parsons was not brought back into the dining room, but I heard opening and closing doors, footsteps along the hallway, steps going upstairs; and concluded Larry was being locked up. I wondered what had happened to Izzie, and if he would help when they locked the hogshead top around my neck. The guards were not chatty fellows. Their forte was to sit. Any move I had made would have been suicidal. My failure with George had put them on the alert. A full hour passed, and another half hour. Ten minutes dragging. Once I thought I heard the far off sound of a motor, but the rest didn't notice it, and I concluded I was mistaken.

Then, with no warning, a single shot sounded, quite a distance away. My guards were instantly on their feet, guns in hand. The parlor door opened and Van Gelder passed through rapidly into the kitchen.

He snapped, "That must be the lookout down at the main road. Get your squad down there as fast as you can, Jenkins."

Jenkins was the man who had captured me, and I found out later the active field commander of the Confidence Corps.

Almost immediately a car left the barn and started down the road in the direction of town. Van Gelder came back through the dining room, glanced at me absent-mindedly, and said to Sandy:

"I won't need him for a while. Take him upstairs to Number 4 and lock him in."

Sandy thumbed me to the door, and I mounted the steep and narrow farmhouse stairs. They had converted the second floor by means of flimsy partitions into a series of small rooms, not unlike cells, in each of which was an iron cot and nothing else. I was fortunate in that Number 4 was one of the rooms that had a window; but it was nailed down and shuttered.

Exhausted, I dropped into bed and lay there thinking and listening. Sandy had gone back downstairs when I was locked in, but there was a guard stationed at the head of the stairs. I could hear breathing through the flimsy wall against which I lay, and taking a chance I said softly,

"Is that you, Larry?"

There was no answer, but almost at once the guard rapped sharply on my door and said, "Cut out that talking."

After a long interval I heard the car returning along the road, and sounds from below which meant only confusion to me. Then I must have dozed and slept fitfully for some hours, for when I woke there was a gray light filtering through the shutters.

An hour or so later there was a clatter of tinware, my door was opened, and a tin plate with a couple of strips of bacon, a chunk of bread, and a tin cup of hot coffee was handed in. It tasted fine, and made me feel a lot better. In the scuffle my wristwatch had been broken, so I had no way of knowing what time it was. I sat on the edge of the bunk, walked around—or rather, up and down the narrow length of the room—and finally lay down again on the bunk. Again, in spite of the order, I spoke with my lips close to the wooden partition, but still there was no answer from the other side, and again the guard pounded on my door and commanded silence. It was a different voice than any I'd heard. I reasoned from the number of men I'd seen and what I knew of the disposition of pickets around the place, and concluded there must be at least twenty men quartered at the farm.

It may have been two or two and a half hours later that there was considerable commotion downstairs; and then I heard a car coming along the road. It chugged wheezily and stopped in front of the house. Quite distinctly someone below my window said:

"Ah, it's the mail," in a tone of relief.

And then, through the partition beside me came Izzie's voice:

"Mr. Moore. Get ready. This is it."

Punctuating his sentence came a single shot, and a fusillade of revolver shots, and on top of that the serried chatter of a submachine gun.

From below came a great clamor and banging of doors, the sound of heavy objects being overturned, men cursed and swore and called excited commands to each other. I yelled, "Izzie! What is it?" And from behind the board came his excited tones:

"It's them! They found out we're here. They've come after us."

I yelled, "Who?" and Izzie called back, "The police!"

On the other side of my room, Jaze Ireton's voice began to call for help, and from somewhere opposite, Larry called, "Jaze! Jaze! Don't worry! Don't be frightened! You'll be all right." Another voice, that of our chauffeur of the night before bellowed, "Let me out!"

Izzie said, "I think the guard's gone downstairs, Mr. Moore. Let's try to get out of here."

"All right," I agreed. "I'll count three, Izzie, and we'll see if we can't break down our doors simultaneously." I gathered myself as far away as I could from the door, counted, One, Two, Three—and charged. The flimsy lock gave, and I crashed into the hall. Izzie's door was made of firmer stuff, or perhaps he didn't hit it quite as hard, for he had to make a second charge. In a moment he was with me.

I said to Izzie, "Now what?" For answer he ran to the head of the stairs, went halfway down, and ducked back up into the hall.

"They're getting ready for a siege," he told me. "They have the furniture piled up against the doors and windows."

The machine gun had stopped, but a desultory fire from pistols and rifles was being kept up from outside. I said to Izzie, "We'd better get Larry and Miss Ireton out of those rooms. Some shots may go wild."

Both Izzie and I looked around for something to use as a battering ram. We solved the problem by pulling the pallet off one of the iron beds, folding up its legs, and using the whole length of it as a battering ram.

Imprisonment had done nothing to aid Miss Ireton's beauty. She had been crying, her face was smudged and her eyes bleary with tears. Her clothes were mussed and wrinkled, but to Larry she was still the Queen of Sheba. Izzie stood by the head of the stairs, with me beside him, both of us expecting at any moment to have the defenders downstairs rush up. But they were too busy to bother. We had made plenty of noise, but the gunfire had drowned us out.

In a lull in the firing, from outside of the house came a stentorian voice:

"Hey there, inside! March your prisoners out, throw down your arms, and we'll let you come peacefully."

From inside Van Gelder answered meticulous and schoolmarmish as ever:

"My dear Lieutenant Tonelli, don't be ridiculous. When we come out, we shall come out shooting, and we will leave our prisoners dead behind us."

15

In answer to Van Gelder's defiance, the police opened fire all around the house. I said to Izzie, "Let's see what we can do with this battering ram on those shutters."

Izzie said, "No, I got a better idea. Let's try the attic and the roof." We found in a corner room a stairway that was little better than a ladder leading through a trapdoor, and went up it expecting every moment Van Gelder would catch us. The roof was shingled, and there was no opening onto it.

Izzie boosted me onto a joist which ran along under the peak of the gables; by standing up on this joist I could reach the roof. It did me no good, and I swung down. There was no escape this way, without tools to break through. Then from the floor below Larry called out and Izzie and I dropped down through the trapdoor. I went first, landing almost in the arms of Sandy. He said grimly:

"Playin' games, huh?" And then stood back, his gun in hand, watching Izzie's fat legs dangle through the trapdoor and kick around for a hold on the ladder.

Another guard had Jaze and Larry and the chauffeur under tow. The five of us were marched downstairs past loopholes in windows where men were standing or kneeling, firing as anything moved outside. It looked as though we were in for a long siege.

"We're going to put you down in the cellar where you'll be safer," Van Gelder greeted us.

There was a terrific explosion at the front of the house, and almost immediately another heavy detonation at the rear. I was facing the front door and saw it quiver, heave and tremble, lift itself inward and upward, only then to go into a mass of splintered wreckage. It had been struck fair by a hand grenade. There was another fainter plop of an explosion, and several others in rapid succession. An acrid, pungent, stinging sensation clogged my nose and throat, my eyes blinded with tears. Van Gelder shouted:

"Tear gas! Watch it!"

Regardless of guards I stumbled forward through the vapor-filled hall toward the front door, and then I lost consciousness of everything but stinging, streaming eyes, nose and throat, until I was out in the open, running toward the barn. Somebody hit me on the shoulder with a sledge-hammer. I spun half around and went down.

WHEN I CAME TO I was sitting with my back up against the wall on the floor of the parlor. Tonelli was bending over me, bandaging my arm with a firstaid kit. My shoulder burned and itched, and I said, with great originality, "Where am I? What happened?"

Tonelli guffawed. "You got a lungful of gas, and then one of your playmates from the house here put a .38 slug through your shoulder." He finished his job of bandaging, strapping my arm to my side with a half-dozen quick turns of wide gauze. Jaze and Larry were across the room, with Jaze clinging to Larry's hand as if she would never let go. Matthew Van Gelder sat with his wrists between his knees, and the bright gleam of handcuffs showing beneath his cuffs. Izzie lounged in the doorway, and a dozen policemen in uniform and out, stood around or bustled back and forth.

"How you coming?" somebody said at my side. That was Bennington Graeme.

I said, "What are you doing here?" And Tonelli answered for him.

"He's the one who brought us to you."

With my arm fixed, Tonelli barked orders until we were left with only Van Gelder, Jaze, Larry, Bennington, the chauffeur, Izzie, myself and a uniformed officer stationed behind Van Gelder. Tonelli had preempted Van Gelder's former commanding position at the scallop-topped table.

Bennington Graeme had ensconced himself on the floor at my side, chattering fast to bring me up to date on events.

"You see," he said, "I was kinda playing possum with you people last night. I wasn't as tight as I seemed to be."

"Yes," I informed him, "I noticed that. I saw you sneaking down the stairs after we had left you. What was the idea?"

Graeme laughed embarrassedly. "Izzie," he said. "I've never trusted that fellow. And, to tell you the truth, you've caused a lot of talk yourself. Nobody knew why you were here, or whom you represented, and how could we be sure you weren't working hand-in-glove with this Fascist outfit? You and Izzie dashing off into the night that way might have been a gag, for all I knew, and so I got in touch with Tonelli, whom I knew for a straight shooter. We had a merry chase following your trail. We missed where you turned off the road, and had to go back and try a half-dozen small side roads. It's a good thing we did, because in the process we found out about this farm.

"Somebody remembered," Bennington went on. "Some farmer down the road had seen that big limousine of yours turn into this road. Tonelli asked questions about the farm, and he and I together with a plainclothes officer searched a part of the way along the road on foot. Somebody took a shot at us."

I said, "Oh yeah. I heard a shot last night. So that's who it was."

"We got away," said Bennington, "and laid low. As soon as it got daylight, Tonelli and his men went on a little scouting expedition. They found this place guarded like the approaches to the Jewel Room in the Tower of London.

"Tonelli decided it was not good business to be seen around the neighborhood. If this was the hangout for the Confidence Corps, we would have to get within striking distance fast, or they would get rid of you prisoners before we could get up to them.

"Then I got the brilliant inspiration of the mail car. This is an R.F.D. route, and this farm is the last farm on the circuit. The farms over on the right pick up their mail on the main road."

"Sure," I said, "I saw a clump of mailboxes when we turned into this road last night."

"That's it," said Benny, "they told us at the post office there was seldom any mail for this farm. Nothing, in fact, except advertising matter now and then. The postmaster and the mail carrier didn't much like the idea of using them for a blind and a decoy, but we finally persuaded them. Tonelli and two of his men with submachine guns got in the back of the mail buggy. It is an old touring car, and there was room for them to crouch out of sight under a tarpaulin. The pickets along the road allowed them to come right through; in fact, Tonelli says he saw nothing of guards. Even when the car got right up to the gate, Tonelli was uncertain this was the place and might have passed on if it hadn't been for the signal in the window."

"What signal?" I asked.

With a wide and proud grin, Izzie Jones came waddling over.

"*My* signal," he said. "The glass in the window in my room was broke, and I stuck my necktie through the slats in the shutters."

"Right," said Bennington Graeme. "Tonelli knew that red, white and blue necktie. There's only one like it in the world—I hope."

"I am going to get a piece and put it in my memory book," I promised, "if Izzie will give it to me."

"Sure," said Izzie, "I'd be proud to."

"Seeing the necktie, Tonelli unloaded from the car; and the minute he showed his nose, the fireworks began. The mail carrier took to the woods, while Tonelli and his two men carried the brunt of the battle.

I said, "They must be three miracle men, because they had this house surrounded."

"Oh," said Bennington, "that was after the shooting started. Tonelli had four carloads of riot squad and State troopers ready to rush in. As soon as the shooting began, they fanned out and surrounded the house. The rest of it you know about."

Tonelli's arrangements were completed to his satisfaction. He said, "Now please let me have your attention," like a stern schoolmaster. "First, we'll hear Miss Ireton."

Jaze came forward, but she never let go of Larry's hand.

"Tell us exactly what happened to you, Miss Ireton, please."

"I was at my Aunt Margaret's house," said Jaze, "waiting for Larry. A car drove up, which I thought was his, but two men got out and came to the front door. They were nice looking men. One of them said he was from police headquarters. He showed me a badge, or rather gave me a quick glimpse of it in the palm of his hand. I've seen so many policemen in the last few days I wasn't suspicious. I've done nothing but answer questions and go places with the police, for identifications and hearings. When this man said he was from Headquarters and I had to come back to town immediately, I took him at his word, went out and got into the car with him. I intended to leave a note for Larry, but we got started before I remembered it. When I said to the man who was sitting with me in the rear seat that I would like to go back and leave the note, he turned on me and laughed. He taped my hands and mouth with adhesive. Then they tied my ankles and laid me in the bottom of the car. One of the men crouched there with me, too."

"That's one of the reasons," Tonelli commented, "we got no word of a car with two men and a woman in it. Pretty slick operators. But not too slick. They should have let you leave the note; then we wouldn't have missed you for hours. Go on, Miss Ireton; what happened next?"

"Nothing," said Jaze. "They drove around for a long time, it seemed to me, although I could tell very little about it. Eventually they brought me here."

"Have you any idea why you were kidnapped?" Tonelli asked.

Van Gelder spoke up.

"You're assuming a great deal, Lieutenant Tonelli," he said. "I demand an explanation of this armed invasion of my privacy. This is a peaceful dwelling house."

"Oh, yes?" said Tonelli. "Lots of artillery around, isn't there?"

"You will find," said Van Gelder icily, "that we have permits for all the firearms here—which I may say are very few. We do a great deal of hunting, and several of our men are enthusiastic marksmen and hold frequent shooting contests."

I touched my shoulder and said, "Somebody scored a bull's eye on me, all right."

Tonelli held up his hand, to silence me, and said to Van Gelder, "Have you got a good story for this snatch too?"

"I resent that term," said Van Gelder. "I resent the implication that there has been any unlawful behavior. First, these men," he indicated Izzie, the chauffeur, and me, "came prowling into my house in the small hours of the night. I had no way of knowing they were anything but common thugs. Then you came with all the armed forces of law, and begin shooting. Now you have the impertinence to accuse me of kidnapping."

Tonelli looked nonplussed. He scratched his head.

"Maybe you're right at that," he admitted, placidly, "maybe when we've heard the story we'll see it's all a big mistake. How come Miss Ireton is here?"

"That is very simple," said Van Gelder. "I asked Miss Ireton here to discuss a matter of family business."

Jaze dropped Larry's hand for the first time and started forward accusingly. "Why, the very idea!" she exclaimed. "You know very well that those men forced me to come here. Why, Mr. Tonelli, I was bound and gagged."

Tonelli looked inquiringly at Van Gelder. "What about it?" he asked.

Van Gelder laughed. "Ridiculous," he asserted. "I'm afraid my young cousin is a trifle hysterical. She was not bound; she was not gagged. I can prove *that* by the two men who brought her here. They're friends of mine. I simply asked my cousin to come here in order that we might talk in some privacy."

"I see," said Tonelli slowly. "I guess Miss Ireton is a little bit overwrought. That happens, sometimes. People who've been through a lot of trouble begin to think the whole world's picking on them. Maybe Miss Ireton imagined a lot of this."

Jaze blazed like a rocket. "Imagination?" she cried. "Look." She exhibited the marks of adhesive tape.

Van Gelder maintained his superior attitude.

"After all," said Tonelli, "it seems to come down to a question of your word against Miss Ireton's, Van Gelder. You say you have men who are prepared to back up what you say."

"Certainly," said Van Gelder.

Tonelli smiled. From his inside coat pocket he produced an envelope, and from the envelope he removed a tiny, raggedly-triangular bit of paper. He held it up so that Van Gelder might see it.

"What have you to say about this?" he asked.

Van Gelder stared at the tiny scrap of paper. "What have I to say about what?" he was apparently as much puzzled as the rest of us.

"You see," said Tonelli, "I'm just a cop, and cops are dumb. I'm no fancy detective. The only advantages we cops have on our side is that there's a lot of us, and we can take plenty of time to do things thoroughly."

He leaned back in his chair as though he were about to deliver a long and rather dull lecture.

"Now in your case, Mr. Van Gelder, I thought I had you all lined up for a kidnapping charge; but you're too smart for me. I'm always forgetting I'm a cop, and dumb. I come busting in here with machine guns, I'm breaking into a peaceful farmhouse where a gentleman is having a little family conference. I don't even know until right this morning that you are Miss Ireton's cousin."

I could contain myself no longer. I called out:

"You see, Pete! That's it. He's not Miss Ireton's cousin—he was Commodore Ireton's cousin. That's what Sarah Hirzner was trying to tell us when she died. We thought she was saying something about the Commodore's 'cussin'.' But she was trying to tell us it was the Commodore's *cousin*, who did the murder."

Van Gelder turned on me.

"Very ingenious," he said, sneering. "I've noticed, Mr. Moore, you are fond of bad puns."

Tonelli waved me back. "Let's not get mixed up," he said. "Let's take things one at a time. Right now I'd like to know what Mr. Van Gelder has to say about this little scrap of paper."

"I've nothing to say about it. What could I say about it?" Van Gelder demanded. "Looks to me like an ordinary fragment of plain white paper."

"That's all it is," said Tonelli, "just a little piece of paper. Nothing on it. No fingerprints. No printing, no writing, no blood. Nothing. It's a hell of a clue. One of these great detectives would laugh himself to death over it. But you see, that's an advantage of being dumb. When you're dumb you don't know when to laugh. This little scrap of paper came off Commodore Ireton's desk."

Van Gelder shrugged.

"Okay," said Pete, "so what? I'll tell you what. There were a whole stack of reports on Commodore Ireton's desk. There was a couple of inkstands, some pens and pencils, and two or three scratch pads;

but this little scrap of paper was the *only* piece of torn paper on that desk."

Van Gelder said, "Remarkable."

"It was," said Tonelli. "Commodore Ireton was a very neat man. He didn't scatter paper all over the place. He didn't tear up papers. He crumpled 'em up, and dropped 'em in the wastebasket. He didn't break string: he cut it with a pair of shears, and he dropped *that* in the wastebasket. He had the wastebasket right at his side. Right alongside of his chair. And there wasn't a torn scrap of paper in the place, except this one."

Van Gelder yawned. "This may be all very pleasant to you, Lieutenant," he said ironically, "but I am not used to handcuffs and I find these other irrelevancies irksome. I would like to get into the city and go through whatever formal proceedings you may deem necessary in order that I may get in touch with my attorneys as quickly as possible."

"My goodness," said Tonelli. "Here you are, a good citizen. You obey the law, even to the extent of getting permits for your guns. But you fuss because we want five minutes to get a case straightened out. Now Mr. Van Gelder, I want your cooperation as a citizen. How about it?"

"I'm always glad to cooperate with the police," Van Gelder met sarcasm with sarcasm.

"I'll come to the point as quickly as possible," said Tonelli. "The Commodore was as neat and tidy as it was possible for a man to be. Seems probable, then, that if there was a torn scrap of paper on his desk somebody other than the Commodore tore it. Unless it was an accident."

"That sounds reasonable," said Van Gelder. "Even the Commodore could have an accident."

"That desk was piled high with reports," Tonelli continued. "All of these reports were typed on Government paper. This scrap of paper is Government bond too. Question is, where did it come from? We looked and looked, and there was no sign of any other scrap of torn paper. Then one of the bright boys at the laboratory noticed something under the microscope. If you'll look at the corner of this paper, you will see that it is smooth and slightly curved. Now you are familiar with ring binders, aren't you, Mr. Van Gelder?"

"Certainly," said Van Gelder.

"Your report was in a ring binder, wasn't it?" Tonelli asked him.

"As I recall it, yes," said Van Gelder.

"Now I'll show you a funny thing," said Tonelli. From his pocket, the same pocket from which he'd produced the envelope, he brought out several folded sheets of paper. They were all blank, each of them had been perforated with three holes about ¾ of an inch from the edge for a ring binder, and each of them had a neat little triangular tear extending from the extremity of the top hole to the edge of the paper.

"You see what we did," Tonelli explained. "We perforated a lot of paper, and we put it in a ring binder; and then we tore out sheets from the middle. About one in three tore like this one." He held up a specimen with its triangular tear. "In other words, Van Gelder, *you* tore out a sheet from *your* report that was in front of Commodore Ireton when we found his body. You were in a hurry, you had to work fast. You'd just killed him. You wanted to get away from there quick. You never noticed that you left behind this little scrap of paper."

Van Gelder laughed harshly. "That's ridiculous," he said. "*My* report was *not* in front of Commodore Ireton."

Tonelli stood up. He pointed his finger directly at Van Gelder.

"How did you know that?" he demanded.

Van Gelder leaned back in his seat. He paused a long moment before he answered, and his voice was steady when he did reply.

"Why, I saw the desk after the Commodore was dead. Everybody who was present saw the desk. All the people who were there for the conference."

Tonelli turned to me. "Did you notice whose report was in front of Commodore Ireton?" he asked.

I said, "Yes, it was Mrs. Flood's report."

"Exactly," said Tonelli. "Van Gelder's report was buried in the middle of a large stack at the side. All the reports in that stack except Van Gelder's were engineering department records. The reports immediately in front of Commodore Ireton were the reports of the people who were in conference with him at the time of the murder. All but Van Gelder's. And there's another funny thing about it: it was the only report in the whole lot on the desk that had a sheet missing. We dumb cops found that out—and it took us a long time—because we had to go through every report on the desk; that's the reason we kept that room locked up, and kept a guard there. We went over everything in the room. Van Gelder's report had a page missing, and there was this scrap of paper. Not only that, but there were two other copies of this report in Van Gelder's office files, and the same page that was missing from the one in the Commodore's office was missing in each of the copies."

"It seems to me," said Van Gelder casually, "as if the police had gone to a great deal of trouble to detect a clerical error. It is quite obvious to me that some clerk failed to bind one page in each of the reports. Probably in copying they skipped a page. That happens. Our office help is not as good as it might be."

"But we did some more checking up," said Tonelli. "We found that the page missing was from the part of the report that had to do with the work of the researches at the Hall of Records. That page of the report was almost a complete report of a week's work of the man whose dead body we found in the river."

"Remarkable coincidence," Van Gelder sneered. "Are you going to make a charge of murder against me based on silly stuff like this? What will a jury say about it?"

"What about the will?" Tonelli asked.

"What will?" countered Van Gelder.

"Your grandfather's will," said Tonelli. "Didn't your research man discover a long-lost will in the files at the Hall of Records and tell you about it?"

Van Gelder rose to his feet. "This foolishness has gone far enough," he said. "I demand advice of attorney before we go any further with this nonsensical questioning."

"All right," Tonelli conceded. "You have no objection if we ask Miss Ireton some questions, have you?"

"Miss Ireton is a free agent," said Van Gelder tartly.

"Do you know anything about a lost will, Miss Ireton?" said Tonelli.

"Why yes, something," Jaze said slowly. "It's been a family leg-
end, you might say. Claes Van Gelder, who was my father's grandfather—and Matthew Van Gelder's grandfather, too—was supposed
to have left a will. But nobody knew where this will was, and we all
suspected a great deal of the property had been lost. Some time before my father's death he told me one night he thought he had got
on the track of the will. Cousin Matthew had his men working in the
city records. One of these men had found a copy of the old Claes Van
Gelder will, which had been filed for probate, although the original
was gone, my father said; and he also told me Matthew was bringing
the will around to show it to us. I forgot about it. In the excitement
and the horror of my father's death I didn't give it another thought
until Cousin Matthew called me after father's death and asked me
some questions about papers and things. He told me that he had
shown the will to Father. He said he had given Father a copy of it,
and asked me if the copy was in the house. I told him it was not."

Tonelli said, "Then you never saw this copy of the will?"

"No," said Jaze.

"You didn't think to say anything about this will to the police, did
you?" said Tonelli.

"No," said Jaze, "but when I heard through Larry that something
had been taken out of Miss Hirzner's apartment that might have
been a legal document, I began to think about the will, and began
to wonder about it. I called up Cousin Matthew and asked him if it
was possible the will could have been in Miss Hirzner's apartment.
He was very short and nasty to me over the telephone. He said it was
impossible, and that I was a very undutiful and ungrateful daughter
to be blackening my father's name by recalling the scandal attending
his death and that of Sarah Hirzner."

Tonelli looked in my direction, and it was a very dirty look. He
said, "It's too bad there were so many amateurs involved in this case.
The existence of that document as a clue was supposed to be a police
secret."

I said, "Have a heart, Pete. I didn't discuss it with anybody except Larry and Bennington Graeme. And if I'm not mistaken, you
brought up the matter yourself to two or three people."

"Skip it," said Tonelli, "Go on, Miss Ireton."

"Well," said Jaze, "my cousin's attitude made me feel more than ever there was something funny about the will, and I decided to talk it over with Larry. I never had a chance though. Yesterday when I was brought here Cousin Matthew questioned me for an hour about the will and was very insistent about knowing if I'd told anyone about it."

"That lawyer we picked out of the river," Tonelli said, "probably knew a little bit too much about the document too."

"Did your cousin *say* anything to you about *why* you'd been kidnapped after you arrived here?" Tonelli asked Jaze.

Jaze said, "Yes, but it was in a funny way. He rather gloated over me. He said curious things about my father. He said Father 'wouldn't get ahead' this time. I don't quite know what he meant. Cousin Matthew has always been a little jealous of Father. My father was a successful man, and Cousin Matthew always resented that. But certainly it would never have occurred to me he would do my father or me any injury. He always pretended gratitude to Father because of the position Father had given him, and other help he had received from Father in the past."

"Then you know nothing more about the contents of the will than what you've told me?" Tonelli asked.

"I know nothing at all about the contents of it," said Jaze. "I only knew it had been discovered."

"Well," said Tonelli, "you'll be interested to know that not only has the will been discovered, it is in the files of the Hall of Records, and it gives most of the property contained in your father's estate to our friend Mr. Van Gelder. According to this will, the attorneys at the Corporation Counsel's office of the City tell me, your father should never have inherited it at all. All of the estate should have gone to Mr. Van Gelder."

"Oh," said Jaze, startled. "How very strange."

"Very strange," said Tonelli grimly. "So strange that none of the experts at the laboratory were surprised to find the copy of the will on file is a forgery. It's a good forgery, but we can prove it was not filed when it was supposed to have been, thirty years or more ago. The forged copy of the will is not more than a few weeks old."

16

TWO WEEKS FROM THE DAY I had left there I was back in Washington meeting Ben Cook's quizzical glance over his curved pipe. His office was serene and untroubled. There were no papers cluttering his desk, no guards outside his door, no police detectives bursting in. Only two telephones that persisted in ringing at exactly the wrong spots in the conversation.

"Well?" asked Ben. That question had nothing to do with my health.

I said, "Listen, Ben, you've got me all wrong. My name is Moore, Jim Moore, not Watson. I am not a medical officer late of His or Her Majesty's Service."

"No?" said Ben.

"No," I said. "I tell you it's been pretty embarrassing at times."

"Embarrassing?" asked Ben going into the raised eyebrow's department.

"Embarrassing," I said firmly. "It takes not only native tact, which I have in great quantities, but basic training to enable a man to know exactly what questions to ask, what exclamations to make when the great detective stumbles across another dead body. This is a serious suggestion. I want to put in a word for a new WPA project. An adult training course for detective's stooges. I'll direct the project, I've had experience."

"You might tell me about your experience," Ben murmured. "Your reports have been a little fragmentary lately."

"You've come to the right place for information," I said grimly, "I've found this out about stoogery. The stooge is not supposed to have any ethics or any modesty. He's the guy who spills all so that the great detective can get the credit that is due without getting in wrong with the District Attorney."

"Spill," Ben commanded.

"After our highly dramatic scene in the Confidence Corps' quiet farmhouse," I began, because actually Ben had heard the rest of the story. His bleat about bad reports was just his manner of keeping the subordinates in line. Ben's a good executive and good executives always have to have something about which to complain. "We adjourned back to the city and there I got regular medical attention from a silly doctor who insisted upon doing things to my wound that made it very angry indeed. I can't understand why doctors always have to hurt you five times more than the original injury in the cause of hygiene—"

"Stick to the point," advised Ben.

"There you are," I complained, "I spill my blood for my country but does anybody want to hear about my wound? No one. If it had been an operation— By the way would you like to see it? It's healing nicely now but it's red and purple around the edges and—"

Ben said sternly: "Tell me what happened, or get out. To hell with your wounds."

"Actually," I said, "Tonelli had a peach of a case what with his scrap of paper, the man in the morgue, what he sweated out of Four-Square leaders and—"

"What I don't quite understand," said Ben, "is where Ireton fitted into that Four Square American picture. Was he the leader? Did he start it all? And why?"

"It's really all very simple," I told him. "Actually it all started with Ireton, but he didn't know what he was doing. You see, Ireton was one of those fellows who haven't the faintest conception of the viciousness of censorship. He was a sincere guy. He thought he was right about everything."

Ben said, "Humph!"

"Particularly," I went on, "Ireton couldn't get the idea of the art projects through his head. To Ireton the artists were men on Government payroll, therefore they ought to paint and think what the government bosses wanted. In other words, what *he* wanted. When the artists painted something he didn't understand and told him it was art, he was stumped because he didn't know enough about art to know whether they were right or not."

"Do you?" asked Ben maliciously.

"Nuts," I said. "The writers weren't too much of a problem because Ireton could understand what they were doing. A City guide book. He could see that the musicians made some sense too, although he thought they ought to go stronger on the Poet and Peasant and a little less heavily on Bach and Haydn."

"Shouldn't they?" said Ben.

"How do I know?" I asked. "Do you want to hear this or don't you?"

"Yes," said Ben.

I took that to mean yes he did, and went on.

"When it came to the theatre though, Ireton was all set. You know how it is with a show. Every man alive thinks he's a good critic. Ireton thought he was better than good. Not only that, he considered himself divinely appointed to save the morals of the country. So he suggested that all plays be submitted to him for an O.K. before they were put on."

"What's this got to do with—" Ben began.

"Everything," I interrupted. "Be patient. The Federal Theatre unit didn't see it Ireton's way. They refused to allow him to say what they might or might not produce. That was a matter of artistic technique, they told him, and he had no jurisdiction. Ireton appealed to Washington and Washington upheld the Theatre, in a way. Enough so that Ireton's hands were tied in the censorship move. So he attacked from another angle.

"He called in Van Gelder whom he thought he could trust because Van Gelder was his cousin. He and Van Gelder cooked it up between them to form a sort of vigilante committee to watch the Federal Theatre productions to see that they did not put over any Red propaganda in their plays."

"Nice idea," murmured Ben.

"Fine," I agreed, "only it didn't work so good. The Federal Theatre put on exactly what the director wanted, and on the whole it was pretty good stuff. However, from the vigilante committee Van

Gelder got an idea. He organized his Four-Square patriotic society. Pretty soon it was going strong. It got going before Ireton really knew what was happening. When Ireton saw the fine Fascist nest he had fostered he got scared. He tried to call it off, but by then Van Gelder thought he was too strong."

"So Ireton got killed because—" Ben guessed.

"Don't jump at conclusions," I warned, "It was not as simple as that. Consider Van Gelder for a minute. Here is a guy who has had what he calls hard luck. He was smart, but he had never been able to make a success. He actually needed a WPA job when Ireton put him to work. With this Four-Square organization Van Gelder got his first taste of power. It went to his head. He created the mysterious General Z. Van Gelder was Z. He was also the Messenger. He was the works. He got ambitious. He began to figure how he could get into big money fast. The most money he could think of lying around loose was Ireton's estate."

"I begin to see," said Ben.

"Sure you do when I draw you a map," I told him. "I see too, now. The Van Gelder and Ireton family, like all families, had these family stories and traditions. There was that story about Claes Van Gelder's lost will for instance. Van Gelder took that as a start. First he ordered his research lawyer to find the will. There was no will. Then Van Gelder decided that it would be a good idea to forge a will. He did. He had his research man plant that will in the City archives."

"Good idea," said Ben.

"Swell," I admitted. "But Van Gelder made a mistake. He told Ireton the will had been found on such and such a day. He also gave Ireton a copy of the will. Ireton took the copy and looked it over and decided it was a fake. He waited his chance to prove it. When Van Gelder submitted his report, Ireton went carefully over the report and discovered there was nothing in the record that would indicate that Van Gelder's research man had found the will or any other similar document on the day Van Gelder said it had been found."

"It's a smart man who knows how to use reports," Ben commented.

"Not so smart in this case. It got Ireton a one-way ticket to wherever he went," I said. "Unwisely, Ireton told Van Gelder before the meeting of the supervisors that he had found this discrepancy. When the rest of us rushed out to see the riot, Van Gelder and Ireton took the opportunity to continue their private family quarrel. Now see the situation. Van Gelder was in deep. Ireton wanted to get rid of him. Ireton wanted to get rid of the troublesome Four-Square organization and with Van Gelder out of the way that pleasant society would fade.

"Ireton probably thought that if he could make this false report of Van Gelder's stick, he could fire Van Gelder and dissolve the Four-Square. The two of them went into Ireton's office. Ireton wasn't anxious for a family scandal to come out so he gave Van Gelder a chance to have it out secretly. Van Gelder saw everything vanishing in smoke. He killed Ireton, snatched the page out of the record and thought everything was all right. Where he made his mistake was in thinking that anybody knew anything about the will. He got panicky."

"That's something to remember when you commit a murder," said Ben. "Keep it simple."

"Right," I said. "That's also where Tonelli was smart. He worked on the theory that where a motive for a murder is not obvious, the murderer knows a lot more than anybody else. Also that people who know a lot about any subject always give others credit for knowing more than they do. Therefore, Tonelli searched for a clue that would point to somebody covering up something. Anything. His famous scrap of paper was that clue. Who wanted to cover up the fact there was a page missing from a report? Why should there be a page missing from a report?"

"Why indeed?" said Ben. "Our motto is more and better reports."

"Cut out the sarcasm," I told him. "As soon as my arm gets well I'll give you reports until you yell 'enough.' As I was saying—"

"So you were," said Ben. "All right. I concede that Tonelli is a clever man, but what about the kidnapping?"

"Same idea," I told him loftily. "Van Gelder didn't know who knew what. He found out that Jaze knew about the will. He was afraid she would talk. Tell her boy friend or the police or both. He was afraid she had talked before he got around to her. Otherwise he might just have bumped her off and said nothing more about it. Not knowing what she knew or how much she had told, he had to get hold of her and pump her. Get it?"

"But why didn't he kill her when he got her?"

"No time. Things were happening too fast. He didn't know how closely he was being watched. He had to be careful not to be too closely connected with Four-Square. He tried to keep us all, the police included, busy with riots and fights but Tonelli moved in on him by arresting all the ringleaders. We found out by the way that it was not Van Gelder who gave Ireton all the reports and records that were in the Administration office. All the dope on Four-Square."

Ben grinned. "No?" He said, "Who was it?"

"You're asking me?" I said, "You know damn well it was your undercover stooge, Izzie Jones."

"Never heard of him before you began talking about him," Ben denied with a straight face. "What's going to happen to the Ireton girl?"

"She's going to marry Larry, of course," I said offhandedly.

"Tough," said Ben, "and after you went to so much trouble to line her up for yourself."

"The hell I did," I denied, "I never even gave the gal a tumble."

"Just goes to show how mistaken a man can be about another man's motives," sighed Ben. "Now I'd have sworn that the reason you were so eager to go into Ireton's district was because of Miss Ireton. What do you think of that?"

I said, "If that's all you want with me, I'll be stepping out. I've got a date—"

"Fickle," sighed. Ben.

"Listen," I asked. "If Izzie isn't your man, who the hell is he?"

"Why," said Ben, all innocence, "does he have to be somebody's man? Can't he just be an out and out scoundrel?"

"Sure," I said, "he is. Who is he working for?"

"Well," Ben admitted, "I understand his appointment was suggested by a high official in the Treasury Department—"

"I get it, G-man," I said.

Ben shrugged his shoulders. "You guess," he invited, "I don't know anything, except what I read in reports."

COACHWHIP PUBLICATIONS
COACHWHIPBOOKS.COM

THE HEX MURDER

Alexander Williams

COACHWHIP PUBLICATIONS
COACHWHIPBOOKS.COM

THE JINX
THEATRE
MURDER

ALEXANDER WILLIAMS

COACHWHIP PUBLICATIONS
COACHWHIPBOOKS.COM

DEATH
OVER
NEWARK

ALEXANDER WILLIAMS

COACHWHIP PUBLICATIONS
COACHWHIPBOOKS.COM

MURDER
A LA
MODE

ELEANORE
KELLY
SELLARS

CLASSIC RED BADGE PRIZE MYSTERY

COACHWHIP PUBLICATIONS
COACHWHIPBOOKS.COM

PATTERN
IN BLACK
AND RED

FARADAY KEENE

COACHWHIP PUBLICATIONS
COACHWHIPBOOKS.COM

COACHWHIP PUBLICATIONS
COACHWHIPBOOKS.COM

THE MUMMY
CASE MYSTERY

DERMOT
MORRAH

www.ingramcontent.com/pod-product-compliance
Lightning Source LLC
Chambersburg PA
CBHW020647260626
47157CB00008B/2936